IN BROAD DAYLIGHT

IN BROAD DAYLIGHT

A JESS HARDING NOVEL

SETH HARWOOD

THOMAS & MERCER

Text copyright © 2013 Seth Harwood

Published by Thomas & Mercer
PO Box 400818
Las Vegas, NV 89140

ISBN-13: 9781611099720
ISBN-10: 1611099722
Library of Congress Control Number: 2012922339

For Jessica, the original

PART I
ALASKA

CHAPTER 1

It all started again that morning in Anchorage, as it had five summers before. I knew the case better than anyone, well enough that I was called back up from the San Francisco office at the very first telltale sign.

They found her with both wrists tied—barbed wire again. We'd always been careful to keep this particular detail out of the press, our one fail-safe to eliminate copycats, phonies, and wannabes. Too many of the other details were also the same: he'd left writing in blood on the kitchen walls, hit her in the head with a narrow blunt object. This, and it happened during the white nights. Everything with him was always late at night in the summer, when Alaska never got fully dark.

None of the monikers that we invented in the office, or that the newspapers devised to sell copies, seemed to stick. Too many of the patterns would disappear and then pick up again later. The only constant was the blood. The blood, the white nights, and the female victims.

Most of them were young, healthy women—women a lot like me.

This was where I picked up the case again: on a commuter plane north from California, looking through the file and remembering. I hated flying, but what could I do? I wasn't going to drive to Alaska.

Five years had passed since I last worked the case—four summers gone—years when I'd done my best to forget it all, to push him out of my mind, to change the images I saw when I closed my eyes.

Funny thing: it was all just starting to work.

And then the call this morning, the girl's name—Samantha Parker—and my suitcase packed, my ass in the cheap leather seat on Alaska Airlines, and the file folder spread open across my lap.

There were pictures of Samantha as a girl in high school, family photos. In them she was lithe, athletic, vibrant. She looked a lot like how I used to look before the Bureau got ahold of me and turned me into a machine. She ran track; I played volleyball. But her smile was one I knew. It said, "I can beat you."

Then came pictures of her apartment: the blood of a struggle in the living room, writing on her kitchen walls, broken glass, her bedroom, the bloodstained bed. Finally came shots of her body on a coroner's table, the vital and secondary wounds cataloged, photographed, listed.

Behind these pages I found selections from the old cases that I didn't need to be reminded of. I'd committed all the details to memory during that long summer of horrible nights.

Our plane was filled with the same passengers as any other flight into Anchorage at this time of year: hunters, fishermen, tourists bound for a cruise. Locals coming back from their own trips talked across the aisles about places in the Lower 48, confirming the notion that all Alaskans do know one another. I'd refused to believe this at first—until too many of the killings had turned up connections from Homer to Seward to Glacier View and Anchorage. People connected by ways that spiraled and swirled together so no outsider could understand. The longtime Alaska cops had supported me as best they could, but even they started to lose their patience with my questions and the unavoidable cluelessness of an outsider in the strange northern world.

And here I was, going back again, only slightly more accustomed to the Great Land than I'd been at the start of it all.

The businessman next to me—gray suit, briefcase, laptop—tried to exchange glances during takeoff when he wasn't eyeing my legs. Now he tried to make small talk. I shifted the folder away from him, pushing the coroner's photos of Samantha Parker's nude body underneath the pile.

"Heading to Anchorage for work or for pleasure?"

He had the well-fed look of someone going up for work that involved oil, the faint indentation on his ring finger telling me more than I wanted to know. I felt a nagging need to give him the benefit of the doubt. Blame it on my mother, another woman like Samantha Parker who meant nothing but good and got shit for it in the end.

"Just business," I said.

"What line you in?" He craned his neck closer, trying to get a look at the folder.

It was a policy of the Bureau never to talk business with civilians.

"Salmon," I said. "I'm looking to farm-raise coho in the Lower 48." I turned on the fake smile. "There's just so much we can learn from our citizens up north."

I held my breath, hoping he'd stay quiet.

"Yeah, we sure can learn a lot from Alaska, can't we?" He tapped his fingers along the edge of his briefcase. "Lots to learn, and also a lot we can get for our own use, too."

"In your case, oil, I'm guessing."

"Well, that and so much else. If you're interested, I could tell you about—"

I put up my hand to cut him off. The danger in the airplane brush-off is the uncomfortable vibes that last for the rest of the flight, but that's part of why Steve Jobs invented the iPhone. "Save it," I said. "I've got to study this file before we land, and after that I'll be out in the field too much to meet you for a drink. Get me?"

I hit him with my toughest look, one I use in interrogations. At Quantico they called it the Closer. Leave it to the guys there to connect me to Kyra Sedgwick. But I believed in my look all the same.

The businessman blinked hard twice, and then turned back to the window. I took my earbuds out of my bag, plugged them into my iPhone, and turned up Schubert for the last hour of the flight. As I was sticking my face into the file, I couldn't help but notice a look of disdain pass over his face.

So be it.

I could stand to alienate a few people along the way if it helped me do my job. If what I'd seen on this case the first time around was any indication, Samantha Parker's wouldn't be the last of the bodies we would find.

CHAPTER 2

On the ground at the airport, one of the local agents greeted me with a sign and a Lincoln Town Car. He was chipper, well dressed, and ready to serve in that laid-back Alaska way. I rerouted him to Samantha Parker's apartment. The hotel could wait.

Even at nine thirty, the night sky looked like a late afternoon in San Francisco—on its sunniest day. I remembered this part of the summer best: the nights staying light longer and longer, the sun never fully going away. Even after a midnight sunset, the sky never turned darker than a light gray before sunrise a few hours later. Now, in early June, the sun would go down around eleven, fading to a light overcast blue that wouldn't last long.

Summer here was memorable for these nights. And for him. He had made the most of the sunshine.

"Funny thing about this case," my driver said. He was a good-looking kid in his late twenties. Old enough that I'd still look good to him, but young enough that he didn't yet know the job. If he did, the Alaskans wouldn't have picked him to drive me around. He'd introduced himself as Martinez, making him one of the few Latinos in the whole state.

"Funny?"

"Just that this guy makes the rounds of the state, the whole Kenai Peninsula at least, and no one ever tags him with a good nickname. You know? Usually we get a case with three, four murders—less than half what this guy did—and we've stuck him with a name round the office less than two weeks in."

"I know. Major problem for us to work on. Got to get him a nickname." I tapped the top of my briefcase. We were coming into downtown, where Minnesota Drive turns into L Street, and I could see the two high-rise hotels that looked out over Cook Inlet, then beyond them the water and the open land on the other side.

"This guy, his case lasts all summer and then sits on the shelf for five years with no leads, nothing, and we still call him the Writer or the Kitchen Scrawler. What kind of names are those?"

I tried not to take too hard the comment about the lack of solid leads on a case that was my first as lead investigator. It was an insult, but it wasn't clear whether Martinez knew it.

"We toyed with calling this perp the No-Sex Killer," I said, "or the Father Figure, but neither of those kept up with his pattern. That's the problem. His pattern changes."

A car pulled out in front of us, and Martinez laid on the horn, then flipped the driver the bird.

"Plus, you got the whole George Michael thing with Father Figure, too," he said.

"Where you from?" I asked.

"Toledo." He pronounced it like the city in Spain and then laughed. "From the Lower 48's great state of Ohio."

"Maybe you haven't been around enough to get this sense yet, Martinez, but nicknames usually come from the papers, and we just pick them up. So blame the *Daily News* if you want a good nickname for this guy. Otherwise, we'll call this the Parker case for now."

"No, that's cool. It's okay." He waved his hand off the steering wheel. "I actually wanted to float something like the Sunlight Killer by you. You know, that is, if this guy is actually a dude. If he isn't? I'd go with the White Night Widow."

"Nice. Definite ring to that." I looked Martinez over: he was definitely a pup, still wet behind the ears.

"You guys thought about the female angle, right?"

"A few of the local cops liked the scenes as those of a lipstick lesbian slasher flick, but I could never get behind it." We were passing through Delaney Park, a two-block strip of grass that had been a firebreak for the city in the old days. "But you like that idea. What's your theory?"

"I mean, don't get offended because you're a woman and all." He looked my way briefly as we stopped for a red light. His gaze slid over my knees, and I had to stop myself from tugging my skirt down. Tomorrow I'd go with a pantsuit.

I waved a dismissal at any possible offense. "Let's hear it."

"Sure. It's just…I mean, I guess I can just see this being a woman because of the way it goes down. What with the struggle, the style of handwriting on the kitchen wall, these women's backgrounds. You know. All that."

"Sure," I said. "I hear you." I pointed for him to take a left on Ninth Avenue, wanting to get us closer to the water. The thing was, these women didn't have common backgrounds. He hadn't studied the files.

I didn't bring up the backpacking murders that we'd included in this case or any of the details on why they fit. I didn't mention the feats of strength we knew the murderer had to have accomplished during a few of the killings or the walls that he'd climbed. With only one description from afar of the killer having long hair and the build of a woman, and several of the victims being attractive lesbians, some of my colleagues became convinced the killer was a she.

I'd been through enough arguments about this detail, pissed off enough male agents and law enforcement officers, that I didn't want to start in on it again my first night back. "At one point they wanted to pull me off this case because I didn't see it that way, didn't like the female angle. You know that?"

Martinez was quiet as he made a left onto Parker's block. He shook his head.

"I had to fight to stay on this because they said I wasn't seeing things the way a man would." I tried to keep the emotion out of my voice by reading the numbers on the houses. I'd burned more than a few bridges here. For that alone, it was strange they'd called me back to the case. Samantha Parker's father and his position in Washington must have meant they were pulling out all the stops.

In San Francisco, I'd done my best to avoid conflict, even if that meant avoiding relationships altogether. I stayed apart from my contemporaries, other than a few close friends. So here I thought it best to go easy on my driver, keep him on my side. "I know it's a guy, okay? I know this in my gut. Sexy or not, that's my theory."

"I hear you, Harding," Martinez said. He stopped in front of Samantha Parker's building. "And I won't bring up the question again."

He faced me as I looked away from the house. Our eyes met. I didn't like the idea that he was treating me with extra care because of my sex, so I chose to take it as a show of respect for my authority. I was trying to play nice.

"Thank you," I said. I opened the door to the car. "Will you wait out here while I look things over? I like to get a feel for the scene by myself."

He handed me the keys to Parker's apartment. "You bet."

I stood up and straightened my skirt, the keys and my briefcase in my other hand. As I turned to face the building, I looked up at the full height of its flat yellow front. Large modern windows adorned the second and third floors to allow a bigger view of the inlet and the hills on the other side.

I stopped in my tracks, surprised I hadn't realized it sooner: Samantha Parker's apartment was in a building right behind the last one I'd occupied in Anchorage. The two were both new developments, one yellow and one gray, with adjoining backyards, identical in design. They'd been put up by the same developer only a few years apart, and this yellow one hadn't been completed until after I left. That was why I'd failed to recognize the address or place the building when I saw the pictures in the file.

Still, I should have seen it.

Now I stood in front of the building, looking up at a mirror image of my own former apartment house. Both my place and hers had been on the third floor. It felt like more than a coincidence—more like a distant voice calling out my own name.

Jessica Harding, it said. *I'm glad you've come back to play.*

CHAPTER 3

I walked up the path from the street. Every yard here in Anchorage was less than ten feet deep. Less permafrost in front of your house in the winter, less snow to shovel. This was the Alaska way.

Except that Anchorage didn't fit what the locals considered *real Alaska*. Too much city and strip mall, not enough town or village. That, and the nearest range of mountains seemed a little too far away.

I felt the breeze but didn't feel cold in Samantha Parker's front yard. Soon I'd need a windbreaker, something rainproof; but now I felt as comfortable as I had in San Francisco.

The walk ended at three simple steps, and I made my way into the vestibule. Just like my own building on R Street, there was ample room for two people to stand with their groceries in the cold and find their keys while they kicked off their boots. A high bench lined the right wall, leaving enough room underneath for plenty of shoes and boots. To my left I saw a row of mailboxes, the farthest to the right labeled PARKER.

I opened the door onto a carpeted hall, the stairs straight ahead. The sterile scent of new carpet that greeted me had me wondering if the building was even two winters old. If it was, someone was taking very good care of it.

By Anchorage standards, Samantha Parker had been well-to-do. She made more than enough money as a young law clerk and didn't need to draw on her family money from back home in DC, where her father was a three-term senator with a powerful position on the Finance Committee. She would have had roads paved for her along the way and into her current job. If this killing hadn't had the marks of my guy, investigators would have wasted at least a week looking at things from the wrong angle—asking who'd want to get at her father from up here, who he'd upset, and what might make someone jealous enough to kill her for who she was.

But here I was, putting together the pieces of a cold investigation because of a few specific details—markers that couldn't be faked—making my way up the stairs and along landings that looked identical to ones that had been mine. The rugs were even the same light gray, as though the developers had used leftovers to save money. That, too, was just like Alaskans—not wanting to waste resources of any kind.

Samantha Parker's apartment was on the top floor, just like mine. It was a habit I'd developed, always wanting to live as high up as possible, trying to get over the fear of heights I'd had since I was a child. Funny thing about Anchorage: three floors was about as high up as you could go.

The door had the yellow crime scene tape across it, but I pushed it out of the way and unlocked the door. I opened it slowly, trying to summon a heightened attentiveness to whatever I might find. After all the action and bustle of the police officers, investigators, technicians, and photographers, I knew I'd have to concentrate hard to find him. Five years away and now I was back in a place where he'd been less than forty-eight hours before.

I closed my eyes, inhaled, and listened as best I could. My hunches came alive again, but none spoke loud enough for me to hear clearly. I was tired; it would take a good, long, hot bath later—at least—to sort through the feelings of a day spent traveling two thousand miles from where I expected to be and going back through five years of my life to wind up on the same old case.

I kept my eyes closed until I heard a creak behind me. I spun back toward the hallway. But there was no one there. A branch scratched a window.

The blood spatter expert had left taped outlines in the living room, places where the victim had fallen, sustained certain blows, where she'd been dragged. I set my briefcase down next to the door and removed the file. Martinez had given me new pages of analysis, and the blood report was the first I wanted to see. As I read down the list of findings, I noticed a familiar name at the bottom—Steve Owens. So he hadn't left Anchorage after everything he'd said and we'd done. Interesting. I made a mental note to collect on our bet.

Back to the list, I ticked off each item, looking at the tape and the discolored bloodstains. I tried to soak in all the details of where Samantha Parker had been and what had happened in the scuffle. What had he done to her exactly, and where had he stood?

Beside the main chair in the room—an Eames lounge chair with ottoman, vintage and in near-mint condition, worth no less than three grand—the blood spots showed more signs of a struggle. The big chair lay tipped over toward the fireplace. He'd hit her here, I could tell. *I could feel it.* I wanted to hear her scream, but couldn't. Instead, the thud of her head hitting the corner of the couch came softly to my ears.

I saw the blood there, ticked it off on Owens's report. He always did find everything. Then to the floor. Here, she'd been hit hard on the back and side of the head. I looked up and saw light touches of blood on the ceiling, droplets flung from a raised arm as he brought his hand all the way up to drop another blow down on her.

What was it that he used? Owens didn't say. Just a blunt object, with no evidence of it left behind. This would be like the killer, too. Whatever he used, it was the same about half of the time. And whatever it was, we hadn't been able to figure it out.

It would be good to see Owens again, I realized. Maybe I'd even missed him. Beyond whatever we'd had and maybe still had, it would be good to share the details of the case with someone who remembered. He'd be able to help me put the pieces together and remind me if I left anything out. Not that I thought I would, but still.

I wondered if it had dawned on him that this apartment was a mirror of my own. He might have called if he'd realized that. But he'd either missed it or chosen not to give me a heads-up. Neither alternative made sense. Not for the Steve Owens I remembered.

I shook it off; this was no time for dredging up an old romance. I had work to do.

From the living room, the killer had dragged Samantha Parker from the spot on the rug to her bedroom. I followed the carpet to the hall, keeping my back to the kitchen. Whatever I needed to see in there, the pictures in the file were enough for now. I'd be back tomorrow and likely the next day, and when I was here again, I'd have plenty of time to read his bullshit scrawls in blood.

The writing was just to throw us off track. I knew this but couldn't put my finger on how. I couldn't prove it. He wanted to make us think he was crazy, raving mad, but he wasn't. He knew every bit what he was doing, down to the fact that I'd be the one investigating this killing, the one who had headed up his case before. He even knew where I had lived.

For a second I could feel him, imagine where he'd been, what he'd seen. I knew he was somewhere in Anchorage, out there planning his next move, deciding on his next victim.

CHAPTER 4

The bedroom had thick, congealed blood pooled on the mattress. After a day, it had finally dripped down through the bed and the rug beneath it, then the floor and the ceiling of the apartment downstairs. The tenant was another lawyer from the courthouse downtown. The file connected him to oil and pipeline cases. What a surprise. Maybe he knew my friend from the plane. I doubted it. That guy, he'd be in and out before making any local connections.

Blood stained the rug, even past the sides of the bed. A human body contains only eight pints, but those pints could spread across a floor before dripping into and eventually through the wood. He knew what he was doing, this one, always causing enough blood to be spilled on the floor when he was done so that it'd stain and seep. He never wanted it to take too long for someone to find the body, never wanted us too far behind his trail.

That was the kind of sick, twisted fuck I was dealing with again. I hoped I'd be up to matching him this time around.

I shuddered at the thought of the way things had ended on his last spree. Maybe they'd been right to take me off the case, maybe I was better off in San Francisco. But most of it was bullshit politics I wanted to turn my back on: the prejudice of men not used to working with a woman. Maybe this was a second chance—for them *and* for me. This was where I had to be, the case I needed to be working. There was no place else I'd choose.

Her hair had been laid across the pillows, spread out and combed intentionally. He'd taken time at the end to groom her.

Her hands had been positioned carefully by her sides and her fingernails scrubbed and polished clean. I checked the picture and the file again and made sure. This was how we'd found his first victim way back at the start of it all.

Sheila Wells had rented an apartment in a less prosperous part of town. She was one of the women you could see any time of year at the cheap downtown mall, waiting for a bus. In winter, she'd be inside, pressed up against the glass; in summer, she'd be standing outside smoking. All her hangouts had been dives.

Compared with that beginning, our killer had really risen up in the world to get to Samantha Parker. But meager apartment or fancy new one, he'd left the same scene: a woman in her bed, sheets stained red from her blood. Both women had cuts to the wrists from the barbed wire he bound them with, abrasions around the arms from a struggle, and noticeable bruises and trauma to the head from a serious beating with a hard object.

Ugly stick.

The words popped into my mind from writing he had left on a kitchen wall. He took their blood and wrote on walls. The Writer—another name he'd been called. But I'd heard the words *ugly stick* before, back in high school when I was too long and gangly—taller than most of the boys—and wore braces on my teeth. "Who hit you with the ugly stick?" they asked.

I wanted to hit them, take it out on anyone. Instead I saved it for the court and the games. I used it to help us win State.

Samantha Parker had been found flat on her back, plenty of blood around her head and neck to seep through the floor and provide the paint for him to tag her walls.

The cursive writing made some think he was a she, a raging dyke coming after anyone in her circle she didn't like, but this theory was a stretch that didn't last beyond Sheila Wells. She'd gone both ways after a young marriage, met women at Myrna's from time to time, but her real interest was drugs. She'd gotten so deep into crank that she would go home with anyone who was holding.

When she died, she'd been right on the edge: far enough gone to do most anything for a fix but still keeping her own apartment. Not out on the street yet, which was unlucky for her as it turned out.

She was last seen in the park between West Fifth and Sixth Avenues at E Street. Some of her friends remembered her being there, but no one saw her leave. Just a regular white night in the middle of June. Just like the night Samantha Parker was killed. Just like tonight would be.

I put a hand against the wall. These details still haunted me. If I solved the case, maybe they would leave me alone. I hoped.

Samantha Parker had finished work and gone for coffee with a girlfriend to talk. According to the file, she was 110 percent straight. After that, she went to the gym for a cardio kickboxing class and then headed home. No one saw her after the gym, not until our guys found her dead.

I shook my head—trying to loosen up some of the memories or knock them away, I wasn't sure.

Martinez was no doubt getting bored in the car, and I knew I should get to the hotel and settle myself so I could be up early in the morning. Nothing else in the bedroom stood out. Not the dresser, the closet, or anything else, though I'd be sure to give these all a longer look. The shape and layout were identical to my old bedroom, but Samantha Parker had set her bed to face the windows. I'd had mine set to face the door.

Down the hall, her bathroom looked similar to my old one, but it wasn't identical; the fixtures were different: the shower head bigger, the tiles a darker blue. Everything was different but the toilet.

On a whim, I lifted up the heavy porcelain tank cover and felt its weight. What if she had gotten her hands on this and had a crack at the perp? Where would I be now?

I noticed something on the cover's underside. One of the techs had marked in Sharpie where something had been found. ENVE-LOPE, EVIDENCE A17, it read.

I looked through the evidence list in my folder and found no entry for A17, not that that was surprising. Sometimes techs got stuck with too many crime scenes to catalog them all right away. That they hadn't finished the list on the first day wasn't uncommon. If we were lucky, they'd have it done in the next day or two.

But the placement of whatever they'd found made me curious. Taking a closer look, I saw white marks where tape had been. Something had been affixed to the underside of the lid.

He had left one or two notes behind at other scenes—"presents" for us—but not in Sheila Wells's place. Maybe he had, and I just couldn't remember. I made a note to check.

Tomorrow, I'd look in the evidence locker myself and see exactly what the techs had found and what our friend had to say.

I closed my eyes. Though it was just coming up on eleven now, it was midnight back in San Francisco. With my early morning runs, this was later than I usually went to bed. I stepped back out into the hall and looked across the living room to Samantha's kitchen. It could wait until tomorrow.

CHAPTER 5

Martinez was only too happy to take me to my hotel. The Bureau had put me up at the Marriott, just as they always did. In Anchorage the Marriott was the only place to stay worth two shakes of a politician's dick.

I gave instructions to Martinez to pick me up early but then thought better of it and told him I'd meet him at the office or Samantha Parker's whenever he came on the job. I didn't know his hours and didn't want to wait for him any longer than I had to. I wanted to get a jump on things in the morning.

Up in my room, I put my bags by the bed and laid the file out on the table beside the TV. I shuffled a few of the pages around as I got out of my clothes, but before long I was in bed and dead asleep.

That night I dreamed I was trying to cross a shallow river. I was somewhere in Alaska's wilderness, perhaps not the wide-open emptiness that people called the Bush, but far enough out that no one else was around, not a sign of civilization anywhere.

The current was fast, but not too hard to walk against. The rocks underfoot were the hardest part, slick and uneven, jagged in places and unpredictable. I had to fight to stay on my feet, and in the middle of the river I slipped and fell. I caught myself with my hands, and the left landed on a sharp rock under the water. I barely got wet—the water was less than a foot deep—but when I stood up, I saw a dark red cut across my palm. It didn't look good. Blood dripped into the water.

This was the image the dream left me with: my own hand cut open and dripping blood.

When I woke up, I tried to shake that off, but it stuck in my head as I showered and dressed. By the time I checked the clock, it was seven. I decided to walk across town to the Bureau.

Our headquarters for all Alaska took up less than one floor of a nondescript office building on the west side of the city, less than a ten-minute walk from my hotel. In the lobby, you'd never know what was in the building or that it housed anything important. On the first floor was a dentist and an accountant, the branch of a local bank. By the elevator a sign said the third floor held offices for D&I Construction. Nothing out of the ordinary, and you might even understand the folks in suits and ties walking in and out if you thought D&I was running construction for the pipeline to the North Slope.

I rode the elevator up to three and saw the same lobby that I remembered from before. Oil well and drilling posters adorned the walls of a simple waiting room with two wooden doors in the middle. What was unusual began here: The doors always stayed locked. You could open them with a passkey and the slide of your ID badge, but someone inside was watching everything you did and had to manually approve your identity before the locks released.

I slid my ID through the scanner and angled my face up toward the camera hidden behind a small black globe. I smiled wide for it, not knowing who might be on the other side.

The door clicked, and I walked in to see the same drab world of cubicles I remembered. The Bureau didn't go to any lengths to make us feel that our jobs here were glamorous.

"Jess Harding. A blast from the past and a shock to the present. Look who's back in town!"

I turned to see my old partner, Oscar Linstrom, walking out of a corner office with glass walls.

"Well, look who's come up in the world."

He ran his hands back over his slicked hair and held his arms out so I could admire his Armani suit.

"Damn. You getting those shipped up from the Lower 48 now or did they get someone in Anchorage who can sell an actual suit?"

Oscar hugged me and then stood back to get a better look. "My agent! You don't look one day older than the last time I saw you. San Francisco must be treating you *good*!"

He still had his hands around my waist, and it was that or the compliment or both that made my face go warm. Now that I've grown into my height and filled out a little, I get treatment from most men that's the opposite of what I got from the boys in high school. Funny thing is, sometimes it still leaves me feeling the same burn.

"Always the charmer with the ladies, huh, Linstrom?"

"Yes, ma'am." He smiled with the same set of gorgeous whites I remembered.

"Well, good for you."

"Come, come." He led me back to his office and pointed out the cubicles and offices of anyone who'd been around when I was still there. I'd been nervous to see the old place on the walk over, but now I felt glad to be back.

It was still early enough that none of the others I knew were in yet. Just a couple of newbies sat at their desks drinking coffee, catching up online, and trying not to look as if they wanted to know who I was or why I was here.

All agents try to act mysterious when they start on the job, trying to emulate their favorite sleuths—we all have a favorite we really want to be, and no, mine's not Nancy Drew—but we all have to learn the ropes. The single biggest fact about investigation is that once you finally stop caring about how you look, that's when you become inconspicuous. Not caring led to some of the best work in the field. Strange but true.

Another truth: my desire to be perfect, the drive that made my life awkward all through high school and college and has ruined more dates than I can count, fits right in here, even helps me do the job. It still doesn't translate to a life outside, but it works while I'm on a case.

Linstrom brought me into his office, and I gave him the quick facts about my world in San Francisco. No major boyfriends, a decent apartment, swimming and hiking and long bike rides to stay in shape. Travel wasn't too bad; most of our cases weren't out of the ordinary. In short, it'd been a good five years.

"And now you're back for the Writer case again. Your old friend."

I laughed. He knew enough about what I'd been through with this case to know I could have passed on the chance to come up. And now he knew I didn't pass. Instead, I got on the next plane and hit Samantha Parker's apartment late last night. He knew I was all in.

But I didn't know what he'd make of that.

Outside his window, it was sunny. Had been when I went to bed and was when I woke up. You had to love this time of year in Alaska. Even if it did inspire a killer.

Finally Linstrom smiled. "We got a break last night on the case. A possible witness."

CHAPTER 6

A man had come in to the police station late the night before, just around the time I was inspecting Samantha Parker's apartment. After seeing her picture and the story on the evening news, he only took a couple of hours to talk it over with his wife and realize that the right thing to do was to call the police.

Your average Alaskan's distrust of the law kept more details out of our files than you would believe. A couple of hours' pause actually made this guy a saint. If he'd known that the real interest in this case was federal, or if the news report hadn't suppressed the information about her father being a senator in the Lower 48, he'd likely never have come in. Distrust of the federal government and animosity toward the lower states were generally bred into Alaskans, even before their respect for the cold.

Nevertheless, this Willy R. Nelson—no relation, name change, or acknowledgment of alternate spelling—had come in to the police station last night around ten, given his report, and within an hour found himself in the interview box with three federal agents.

"And I wasn't notified of this as it was happening? Why's that, Linstrom?"

"Shit, Jess. We do things different up here. Takes a few hours for things to get through channels. You know."

I nodded. It was bullshit, but there wasn't much I could do about it now. Linstrom brought me into the viewing room and started the tape of Nelson's interview. I saw a tired-looking postal clerk sitting at a plain Formica table. He wore a red plaid shirt but didn't have long hair, braids, or a beard. A few gray hairs were gathered around his temples, and he sported a bushy mustache just as brown as the table was white.

Linstrom said, "Wasn't like he gave us a lot."

He let the video play from the beginning. Nelson sat talking to a couple of homicide cops, who started off with routine questions about why he'd come in.

He said, "I think I was the last person to see her alive."

More particulars. I could see from five minutes of watching this man talk that he was telling the truth. No signs, no tells. I was the one who beat the other agents when we played poker. They said I was born to spot a liar, and that or the way I took their money usually led to me not being invited back. I'd learned to live with it.

Linstrom started fast-forwarding the tape as soon as one of the cops got up. This would be when he left to call us.

"What do you think?"

"He's telling the truth," I said. "And I want to go see him."

I stood up from my chair and checked the clock. Just after eight a.m., and that meant the day had technically begun—time to visit a witness.

Linstrom kept fast-forwarding the video. The other cop came back, and they both left. "Don't you want to see—"

I cut him off. "I want to talk with this one myself."

Twenty minutes later, I stood on Nelson's doorstep. I knocked. Two things had helped me make it that fast: First, Linstrom had been kind enough—or interested enough—to give me a ride. He wanted to watch what I was up to. Second, even at the rush hour of eight in the morning on a Friday, you could make it across Anchorage in less than fifteen minutes—even without a highway.

A stout woman answered the door after a minute, and I could tell from her jeans and sweatshirt that she'd been awake. She had one work boot on and laced up, the other on but with the laces dragging to the sides.

She took one look at us and sized me up even faster. "Feds," she said in a scratchy voice. If she'd been a smoker for four packs, she'd been one for four decades, at least. "You here to see Willy, I expect."

She showed us in and offered us coffee. I accepted but cringed when I saw the tall jar of instant Folgers on the counter. Even a month in San Francisco could turn you into a coffee snob. The first friend I made in the Bay Area office, Marlene Roberts, started taking me out afternoons and got me addicted to lattes. I blame it on her. Here in Alaska, even Starbucks had yet to catch on. A cappuccino was something beamed in by aliens.

Linstrom smiled as Ruth Nelson set the jar, a spoon, and a mug of hot water in front of me. When she'd turned to get her husband, he said, "Priceless, Harding. If you could only see your face."

He reached for his pocket, and I flinched, expecting him to be pulling out a smartphone to snap my picture. Instead he came out with an old-fashioned flip notebook. He made a note there for himself. "Just a quick note to remind myself to tell this one later on."

"Great. Thanks."

"Let me guess. Double-shot, slow-drip French press macchiato?"

"You bet. With soy milk." I spooned in a heaping tablespoon of crystals and eyed the powdered creamer. "Push me that sugar, will you?"

Linstrom tried to look hurt. "*She never has a second cup at home.*"

I heard a commotion in the back of the house, and then Ruth Nelson came back. "Says he's tired. But he'll be right out in a minute."

She got her coffee off the counter and gulped it, munched a piece of toast. "Beg pardon, but I got to be off to work." She pointed to the coat rack with her mug, and I saw a yellow vest and construction helmet. "Road crew on the Glenn Highway. Called in late, and they give me eight thirty. Praise 'em."

She passed behind me as I saw her husband rustle across the hall into the bathroom wearing striped boxers and a yellowed undershirt, and pulling on his robe.

"He called in sick. Saying he's traumatized from all the talk last night with you folks. I give him one day and the weekend. Come Monday, he's back at that job, you bet."

She pulled on her vest without setting down the coffee or toast. Then, after she put the last bite into her mouth, she reached out to shake my hand. "Good to see a woman wearing a suit," she said. With that, she flipped her helmet onto her head and walked out.

"Thanks," I said when she was gone.

Linstrom sucked at the side of his mouth. "I love me this land here," he said.

My coffee had a thin film of grease across its top and steamed meekly. "Do me a favor and throw this out?"

The toilet flushed, and Nelson walked into the hall, pawing a pack of cigarettes out of a robe pocket. He shook one up and mouthed it. Once in the kitchen, he flipped a stove burner to life and put on the kettle, leaned down, and lit his cigarette off the flame like he'd practiced that move more times than he'd cooked an egg.

He squinted through his inhale and sat down across the table. "Ruth says you here to talk about what I seen the other night. Don't expect me to have invented or misremembered anything new."

"Fair enough." I tapped my fingers along the sides of the coffee mug that Linstrom hadn't had time to empty. "I'm Agent Harding, and this is Agent Linstrom. I just want to ask you a couple of questions."

"Shoot," he said. "But not literally." He smiled.

I warmed him up and got the basics as his water reached a boil and he made his coffee—black without creamer—and started to sip. He smoked away, ashing into a glass dish at the center of the table half full of last night's butts.

"Just walking our friends' dog for them over along the old fire-break. They're on vacation is why."

Linstrom looked around for the dog. "You didn't want to bring him back here to stay?"

"She's a girl," Nelson said. "And huh-uh. Not that yapper." Another sip of coffee, another drag of his smoke. "Anyhow, 'bout ten, ten thirty two nights ago this was, and I seen this girl walking, pretty you know, and a car come up on her from behind. Seemed strange how slow it moved, but I didn't think much of it. When he stopped and said something, she all stiffened up like something was wrong. But what could I do? She shook her head, talked for a few, ten seconds maybe, and then goes around to the other side of the car. She got in. Now I know something about this, I expect he might have had a gun."

"Did she act surprised? Look like she might try and run?"

"Don't know how she acted or looked. Dog pulled on my arm, then next thing I seen she was getting in the car."

"Did you see the driver's face at all, Mr. Nelson?"

He shook his head. "Not real good. Just enough to tell you he was a white fella. Brown hair, most likely, but that's about all I can say. And Lord knows that's not much to go on, not around here."

"You said a man?" I asked. "I just want to be clear."

Nelson bobbed his head. "Sure as I sit here. Definitely a man. Just drove up, said something, and scooped her up right off the street, plain as day. Even if, you know, it was night."

I glanced at Linstrom, gratified that someone had finally verified our suspect as a man. He gave a short nod, knowing what hell I'd been through with the sheriff's department and other agents over the suspect's gender in the past.

"Matter of fact, it was as clear out as you get. Was like he just grabbed her up out of this world in broad daylight, took her clean away from this life."

Linstrom was writing it all down, and I was recording using one of the apps on my phone.

Linstrom said, "You might say she was taken in *broad nightlight*."

I cringed at the pun but tried to hide it.

"No, huh-uh," Nelson said. "Nightlight's like you have for a child to find the bathroom. This just plain as day, like the middle of an afternoon."

He snapped his fingers. "Grabbed her right up. Just like that."

CHAPTER 7

"Broad daylight," Linstrom said when we were back in the car. He hadn't started the engine, just sat flipping through his pad. It was an old habit of ours that we fell right back into, sitting in the car in silence, gathering our thoughts. I'd been going through everything Nelson said, and that was the part that struck me as well.

I said, "Nightlight? Come on."

"You know, like it's night, but—"

"No. He was right. Nightlight is like you leave on in the bathroom at a motel."

"Okay," he said. "I hear you. Call him the daylight killer, then." He underlined in his pad.

"Sure," I said. "Let's drive."

Linstrom started the car. The name wasn't what stuck with me from Nelson's story. It was the way he'd told it, as if something about what he'd seen had left him scared. I first saw it in his eyes on the video but couldn't quite tell then what it was. Now, having sat in his kitchen and watched him smoke his way through the story, I knew I'd seen his fear. It took me a little while to place it on the older man's face; fear isn't something you see too often up here, not when people carry guns on a hike. No, this was a rare thing to see. A man like Nelson, in his late fifties or early sixties, had been through a lot of tough winters, a couple of wars, and plenty of hard times. Walking his friend's dog, a little yippy schnauzer, and something about a random exchange on the street getting him spooked—I just couldn't grasp it.

"Let me see your pad?"

Linstrom handed it over, even as he cruised the pockmarked street: Fifth Avenue was one way in our direction, plenty of lanes and room to drive like a boat coming into a harbor.

I flipped to his last page of notes. "Just want to see how he said that last part, about what he'd felt."

I saw it there in quotes on Linstrom's little page, and when I did I could hear the words echo in my head just the same.

Linstrom quoted from memory, "'Something I could feel from it. Like I could sense an evilness coming off that car and the way he drove.' Not soon I'll forget that line."

Word for word, he'd nailed it. "Then the last part. 'Like it was the most evil I ever known.'"

Nelson said he knew right away when the story came on the news: it was the girl he'd seen and something bad had happened.

We passed the model of the sun that made up the biggest installment of Anchorage's solar system walk.

"Take me to Samantha Parker's, okay?"

I wanted to see the writing in blood at her apartment. I was ready to face it, to get reacquainted with the old darkness, even if it was the same intangible that had spooked Nelson so badly.

CHAPTER 8

Linstrom dropped me off at Samantha Parker's and headed back to the office. As I walked up to the house, I checked my phone and saw I'd gotten a text from Martinez. He'd be on duty in an hour. I texted back my location, and that we had a date with Records.

I wanted to go back and look at the Sheila Wells file. Maybe there was a picture we'd missed, a possible shot to take back to Nelson if I got lucky.

That, and I needed to find Evidence A17.

Inside, the staircase looked even more peaceful and normal in daylight hours than it had the night before. The sun was caught in overcast clouds, and though everything said morning loud and clear, no rays of sun came through the thin windows by the door.

I checked the keys for one that might fit into a mailbox but didn't find it. Someone else would be checking Ms. Parker's mail today, possibly her parents. Her father would be arriving here in Anchorage, coming to see what was what and to mourn. He'd bring press with him, and the story would get a lot bigger. When he came, Samantha's apartment wasn't where I wanted to be. Not in the office either. Anything to stay out of the way of the political machine. Bosses would show up to kiss Parker's ass, trying to make the investigation seem even more professional and detailed than our usual work, which is to say they'd lie, and I didn't want to be a part of that. I didn't want to be trucked out like a display pony to show off a strong woman on the job. They could give you shit all day in the office for being a woman, then when the press shows up you're the face of the whole team. This was a level of bullshit I could do without.

I climbed the stairs to the third floor in silence. Whoever else lived in the building had left for work already. The wind and the foghorn of a freighter accompanied my soft footsteps on the carpeted stairs.

In the apartment, I paused again, as I had last night, hoping to sense something useful. It was an unorthodox technique but one I'd come to rely on during a run of success in San Francisco. In truth, I'd become something of a banner agent since leaving Anchorage, though word of it wouldn't reach this far north. Within my home office, I saw respect in the eyes of my colleagues and felt their confidence. Even if I intimidated a few of the men with my pursuit of perfection, I knew I was earning my keep. That gave me the satisfaction not to care. I worked hard. It felt good, so who cared if I heard the word *workaholic* from time to time.

Now I could feel that satisfaction slipping away as I became a returned version of my former self, an early-career agent with a single major case hanging over her head—a serial killer who had eluded me for a long summer and seven murders, then disappeared as quickly as he had come.

I was ready to see what he wanted to say, what he'd written on the walls of Samantha Parker's kitchen. When nothing new struck me in the living room, I crossed to the kitchen and stood my ground as the image washed over me; it always took a while to take this in.

Her kitchen table and two chairs were huddled together in the center of the linoleum, legs broken off and plates smashed around them. I looked across the field of broken ceramic, happy not to be wearing open-toed shoes.

The kitchen's knives had been pulled out of their block and thrown onto the floor as well. Not in any pattern. Just a mess. I toed forward among the shards, careful not to slip, and entered the room so I could face the wall closest to my left. I'd been trained to go clockwise, starting at the door and moving through the scene as I read what he'd written, making sure not to miss words.

At first, he'd just written garbage: threats, pronouncements, bad poetry, and once or twice even parts of a psalm. But he didn't believe in the Bible; this was no religion nut. Sometimes I got hunches about cases, things I just *knew*, and this was one of them. Down in California, no one ever questioned me. I could proceed head-on, operate on my own. Here in Alaska, I had to fight for every inch of understanding, always challenged by the men around.

This time I didn't care. I would run my own investigation, and anyone who didn't agree with me could run his.

Starting from the left side of the room, the killer had written in Samantha Parker's blood on the cabinets above and below the counter. Most of what I saw there were names, other women I recognized from his last spree. Just first names, never last. Above the counter, fingerprints and hand marks were smeared into the wall. He always pushed any prints around enough so that we could never draw anything useful. When we thought we had something consistent, it turned out to be only partial.

The word *AIDS* stood out to me. I'd seen it before on the pictures of this kitchen in the file and remembered it from one or two of the other scenes. Of course, not all the killings happened in apartments. Some took place in the woods, on popular camping or hiking routes, in public bathrooms alongside one of the state's few highways, and also in hotels. The Traveling Killer was another name someone threw out, also the Tourist, but the newspapers avoided these entirely, attempting to safeguard Alaska's tourism industry, important to the economy as it was.

As I continued my scan around the room, I noted writing on the window. One of our people had affixed a white screen to the outside so the words wouldn't be visible to neighbors or passersby. Then scrawls across the front of the refrigerator and a few lines above it on the ceiling. This killer wasn't always so much a writer as a finger painter. Almost always kitchens. One other time a bathroom wall in a hotel. Otherwise, nothing.

The barbed wire on the wrists. That remained consistent. That, the white nights, and women victims.

Wire was written above the refrigerator. Either he'd used a chair to get up there, or he had to be over six feet tall. Another one of my hunches or suspicions was that he was. Not a giant, but a tall man, well over average height. He'd once climbed an eleven-foot fence behind a victim's apartment, left a piece of his jeans behind at the top. They were standard fare at the Gap. Nothing that could be traced.

Another time, behind a hotel, he got away over a ten-foot concrete-and-cinder-block wall. Sure, there were other ways away, but I *knew* this was his route. The tire marks in the cold mud on the other side of the wall were his, too. Whether we tracked the tire treads and the make, or found a security camera that showed a car driving in or out of a garage, the car was always stolen off the street—not a hard thing to do in Alaska, where people rarely locked their doors. Nelson had seen him in a brown late-model American sedan. It meant nothing to us.

Find me was in his scrawl where Parker had had her dining nook. Behind the table and chairs was more writing. I scanned this top to bottom.

Then I stopped. At its base, just above the floorboards, I noticed one word that chilled my blood. My own name: *Jess.*

CHAPTER 9

I went slowly over the rest of the room and found one more name included in what he'd written: my last name, *Harding*, simply spelled out in block letters right over the sink.

"Shit." I wondered if the other agents had seen it. If that got to the top, I'd be sent back to California for my own protection. They'd move so fast it would leave me spinning. Then I'd be home, watching my back in fear. For how long, I didn't know.

I thought of wiping away the word, using whatever cleaner Samantha Parker kept under her sink and some paper towels to smear it. But the pictures were already in the file. Pictures of everything he'd written. I'd skimmed them myself and not come up with this, missed my own name, but there was a chance someone else wouldn't.

I couldn't take the risk of tampering with the scene. That'd be bending the rules too much to get away with. I'd be off the case before I could say "daylight" and catch a demotion back home in the deal.

No, I'd have to take my chances that no one else would notice my name in all the scratch marks.

"Harding?"

I turned from my own name written to see who'd said it out loud. Martinez stood at the entrance to the room.

"We got to go," he said. "I just got word from the boss that they found another body. This one's down in Homer, out on the Spit. Same scene as the last time there."

"A camper slashed up and left in the water?"

He nodded.

"Shit! Why didn't they shut down the Spit as soon as they knew our man was back?"

I was out of the kitchen and into the living room before Martinez knew I was moving. I bumped him out of my way and took one last look around the apartment, rushing back to the bedroom for anything I'd missed.

I couldn't feel anything new of his presence or see anything worth noting.

Martinez spoke from behind me. "Harding?"

"Yeah." I turned and pushed past him again. "Come on," I said. "We've got to go."

CHAPTER 10

On the way south out of Anchorage toward Seward, I thought back to Sheila Wells, regretting that I didn't have more time to stop and look over her file. I could still see her face and remember her whole story. Something about her made me think of my mother—how she slipped from apartment to apartment for years after she left my dad, always trying to stay one step ahead, running even if he wasn't there. After his drinking went off the rails and he started hitting her, she was never the same. Maybe none of us were.

I tried not to think about it. I always tried.

The drive to Homer would take us down Seward Highway, along the Turnagain Arm until just before Moose Pass, where we'd pick up the Sterling Highway to go west and then south. We'd drive out to the edge of the Kenai Peninsula at Soldotna and then south to Homer for the second body: one Adina Howard, eighteen years of age, found dead and floating. They'd found her in the Fishing Hole at the Homer Spit, a tourist and boating haven with campgrounds, restaurants, and tourist shops. The Spit was also where commercial fishing boats came in to unload. The Fishing Hole was where locals fished for, or rather snagged, anything they could get.

Adina Howard had been snagged; she still had the hook in her when they pulled her out.

Simple, brutal, and illegal to nonlocals, snagging was another way Alaskans made their lives that most Lower 48-ers had never heard of and would never try. I put eating bear and moose into that category as well.

In the simplest terms, snagging means you throw your hook out into the water and reel it in, hoping to hook a fish along its side or in the gills. Then you drag your dinner out of the water. It's not fishing because the fish aren't trying to eat. They're actually just resting. It's the popular method to catch a fish around here because so many of the fish, notably the salmon, have already eaten. They won't bite. And salmon is usually what Homer stocks the Hole with.

The hook in Adina Howard was so big it could haul in a 150-pound halibut. She had it stuck through her ribs and the other end had been fastened to a length of thin wire that was tied around a cinder block. What was strange about the line was that it'd been long enough to let her float. He had *wanted* us to find her.

She'd been beaten about the head like the others, left in the water in the middle of a white night. There were details here that didn't fit, though: no barbed wire at all, anywhere. He'd never left a body without some barbed-wire binding.

As we started the long drive, I tried to get a call in to Linstrom at the office, but my cell phone didn't have service and neither did Martinez's. Though beautiful, the drive south from Anchorage was deadly for both e-mail and cell phone service. As in forget it. Even the satellite radio in most rental cars didn't work. None of the real locals seemed to worry about this or bother to complain. For most tourists Alaska amounted to a foreign country, so if they could use the same currency and their cell phones worked at all, they were happy.

As an agent, I thought it was high time someone found a better way. Local police and many of the people who regularly drove the main highways—truckers and civilians both—used CBs, but our Town Cars had yet to come equipped with them. I couldn't blame the bosses for not requesting them either. Going backward in technology was not an idea those on high would greet with enthusiasm.

The water in the bay and the white-capped Chugach Mountains towering above us gave me plenty to look at. The Seward Highway was one of the two fastest roads in Alaska, where speed limits climbed to a staggering sixty-five miles per hour. If I wanted a nice, calm drive, I'd have been in the perfect place. But that wasn't my mood. Even if I hated heights and the idea of spending an hour inside a small single-engine plane that felt like a can, getting down there fast would be better for the case.

I wanted to see more files, go back through photos from Sheila Wells, talk to other witnesses, find Evidence A17, even hit Homer and get on the ground. But the drive was five hours, at least, with nothing to do.

"Remind me again why we're driving?" I said.

"Budget cuts. Everybody's hurting."

"Really," I said. "Really?" I hit the dash with the butt of my palm. "Alaska's rich with oil money, and they can't get their agents down across a few hundred miles in a jump plane?"

Martinez frowned. He started paying too much attention to his side- and rearview mirrors, avoiding my eyes.

"What?" I asked.

"We're better off not getting into it."

"No, what?" I turned halfway in my seat to face him, my knees up against the center armrest. Today I had pants on, no room for concern about anyone seeing my knees or legs. "Spit it out."

"There's a plane," he said. "We just weren't on it."

"Fuck!" I spun back to the door and hit it with a backhand. "You've got to be kidding."

"Top brass. The bosses want to make this look good for the senator, so they're flying down to get a look. Then they fly back to meet his jet when he arrives from DC."

"Beautiful. Just lovely. No room for my ass on there, even if I sat on one of their laps, I bet."

"Well, if you really—"

"Don't remind me. And a chopper?"

"Huh-uh. Only chopper in Anchorage belongs to the sheriffs, and they haven't let us use that in over a year. State's got money, but they're not into sharing it with Feds."

"Yeah. Just beautiful." I felt like my head had gone on a swivel; I was nodding like a bobblehead. All the bullshit cost cutting drove me crazy when it got in the way of good casework.

I could see the crook of Turnagain Arm out my window, the row of trees on the other side of the water, which meant Kenai Peninsula and a good shot at cell phone service soon.

I turned to Martinez. "You still haven't told me your first name."

He nodded. "It's René. Glad to meet you."

"Thanks for driving me, René."

He winced. "Tell you the truth, I never liked it. Seems like it doesn't fit."

"You could change it, you know."

He shook his head. "Break my mother's heart."

As soon as I had bars, a text message came in from Roberts back in San Francisco. "What's the haps?" she asked. "Where did u go?"

I wrote back, "Alaska. Working old case."

"OK. B careful."

I liked Roberts, but it always surprised me that she cared how I was. I did my best to get the job done, cared most about the case at hand, but she had this interest in being friends—in doing things like drinking lattes in the afternoon. I could see where she was coming from, but it didn't fully compute. The job was what drove me. Getting my man. Relationships? Not so much.

I called the Anchorage office and asked for Linstrom. He wanted to know how the drive was going—all this concerned interest all of a sudden. I could hear in his voice that he expected me to start bitching about the plane.

"Not touching it," I said. "I'm a whole new happy camper now. No complaints out of me. You men are fifty percent of the best of our species."

"Sure. Sure. I bet you just got finished ripping them a new one when you found out why you were on the road."

I looked at Martinez. He probably couldn't hear the whole conversation, but he'd gotten enough sense of it that he had a smirk on his face.

"Yeah, I got it out of my system."

Linstrom had a good laugh, but I cut him off with my request for the files on Sheila Wells.

"What?" he asked. "You want me to fax them down?"

"Fax, e-mail, whatever you got. Just get them to me."

"This is Homer you're going to. They haven't had as much as a Kinko's there. Ever."

"Find *some*thing," I said. "Do me this one favor."

"Yeah. I will for you, Harding."

"And one more thing," I said, "I want *all* the pictures. And *all* the evidence from Samantha Parker's. Especially A17."

CHAPTER 11

An hour later, we were passing Soldotna, the point where the Sterling Highway turns south.

"Second killing in 2006 was here," I told Martinez. "But that was a full week after he killed Wells in Anchorage. He's picking up the pace this time, covering more ground. He didn't get to Homer last time until number four."

"It doesn't make sense. How'd he get down here this fast?"

"Unless he had a plane."

"Yeah, right."

I let that sit for a while, watching the trees go by, feeling as if something was off.

"The third killing last time was in Ninil-something," Martinez said. "Or Nikolisk. I've been reading the file."

"Ninilchik," I said. "That's where the third body was found. Nikolaevsk is the Old Believer settlement down here. If a girl turned up dead there, we'd be lucky if news of it even got out."

"They're the crazy Russians?"

"Kind of. These people trace their way of life back to an old sect of the Russian Orthodoxy that split from the main strand in the seventeenth century. In their world, sixteen is prime marrying age for a woman, and AK isn't an abbreviation for the state; it's the gun they like to carry. The Old Believers make most Alaskans look like New Yorkers."

We passed wooden statues of salmon, eagles, and bears that had been carved with a chainsaw. These were set up alongside the road, with a big drive-thru espresso vendor behind them. I wanted to ask Martinez to stop but didn't. I could hold out.

"I still get those *N* names mixed up."

"For me it's the mountains." I watched the trees pass by out my window. Just beyond them, I could see water and then far off behind it a range of mountains that wasn't the Chugach. I couldn't remember the name of this range or many of the ranges in Alaska. There are just too many to keep track of.

As I thought back to the old cases and what I wanted from the files, I began to speculate about Adina Howard. I hoped the other special agents would be gone by the time we got down there and I could have the crime scene to myself. Same for the body. There would be some kind of message in it all, of that much I was sure. Something was changing. Something was new.

I watched a moose alongside the highway, standing in among the tall grass and munching on leaves from a yearling tree. He couldn't have cared less about our presence as we drove past him.

Martinez pointed him out. "Moose!"

"There he is," I said. "Right where he's supposed to be."

The rest of our drive to Homer was uneventful, and I dozed off against my window. On the clock or not, coffee or no, put me in a Town Car and the scenery can be as beautiful as you like, I'm going to doze off. It's a fact. Get me in a standard San Francisco car like a Prius or something small like that, and I'm too cramped. Not for these legs. But in the Town Cars we drive for the Bureau, I do just fine.

I woke in Homer, where we drove straight through, taking the main road's one turn as it goes from the north end of town to the Spit at the south. We passed the McDonald's, even though Martinez wanted to stop. I remembered a local telling me on my last trip that they'd banned all chain restaurants back in the eighties, but since the McDonald's was already there, they grudgingly grandfathered it in.

At the Fishing Hole, a few of the hard-luck locals stood around disgruntled that fishing was off-limits until we completed our work. The Anchorage brass had finally finished up and flown back to meet Senator Parker, but now here I was with a hungry-looking Martinez, ready to conduct my own investigation that would keep them from fishing for another few hours. These weren't just avid fishermen; they were looking for their dinner. If they had anywhere else to be or a boat to get on, they'd have been long gone.

"Any of you see anything last night?" I asked, just to let them know where I stood in the pecking order. The brass had probably canvassed the crowd already, but it didn't hurt to check.

"I just seen her floating," one woman said. She was on the backside of fifty and had been out in the sun quite a bit. "Come up on her this morning. I reported it. Wrecked up a good day of fishing is what I really did."

I stepped away from the car and led her gently away by the elbow. "Have you talked to any of the other officers here today?"

She shook free but continued to walk with me away from the others. "Sure, I spoke to the police here in town, but none of your suit buddies asked me, so I didn't say shit to 'em."

"Would you like to tell me what you found?"

"Just saw that body out there in the water, like I said. Right on about six a.m. Knew it was a woman and could guess she didn't have any clothes. Thing like that, it's not only awful, but it's bad for the fishing. Plus"—she looked around—"you let these horndogs see a naked lady, even a dead one, there's no telling what they do."

She had clear eyes and a face that showed hard drink. I thought of my father the last time I saw him. Up here it could get even worse. Sometimes, I'd see people who had gone far deeper into some other drug—meth or smack—and their faces looked hollow, like something had changed the shape of their skull and pulled the life out of their eyes. I've heard them referred to as tweakers, but zombies is closer. I saw a pair of them sitting across the road, smoking and watching, waiting like vultures for us to go.

I took the woman's name and gave her ten dollars. "This'll help you get what you need for the day."

She nodded and thanked me. I asked her where she was staying, and she pointed to a row of tents along the other side of the road, out on the far beach. The wind was blowing in hard from that direction, off Kachemak Bay and beyond that through a string of tall, jagged mountains topped with snow.

"You see anyone around here this morning or last night who looked suspicious?"

She pushed out her lower lip and drew her chin from one shoulder to the other. "Nope."

"You ever see her before?"

Same reaction. I thanked her and headed back to Martinez.

She walked across the street with her ten dollars, headed toward a string of small shops that had a fast-food restaurant I hoped she'd go into. The liquor store was more likely, so I didn't watch.

"There's a diver down," Martinez said when I came up beside him. "They already harvested up whatever was attached to the body, but now they're down giving it a last look-over to see if they can find anything else."

"Might as well."

A local officer stood by himself, looking out over the water. I guessed he was supervising the operation.

I pointed at him with my thumb. "He say where we can find the body?"

"Gave me directions to the station. They got a coroner there as well as the morgue. All-in-one service, so to speak."

He didn't look at me as he spoke. Instead he watched the water in the Fishing Hole. At its mouth, the land closed to two points not ten feet apart. Though the view above this was spectacular, that wasn't what Martinez saw.

"You all right?"

"Just the water," he said. "This woman killed and left in the water. It makes me feel cold. You know how long we'd last in water at this temperature?"

I told him I didn't, but I guessed it wasn't a lot of time.

"Thirty seconds, not even. Your heart would stop before you even had the chance to drown. Just from the shock of the cold."

"Not here along the shoreline. You'd have a chance for a little bit. You're thinking of what it's like out there." I didn't know the truth of what I was saying, but Martinez looked away from the water then, and I could see some satisfaction in his eyes. Whatever he'd heard, you couldn't walk around all year in Alaska fearing the water. What did that get you?

I pointed out the restaurant across the street and suggested he get his lunch there while I called back in to Anchorage to see where Linstrom had sent my file. Of course the police station would have everything I'd need—fax, e-mail, printer—and I should have thought of that sooner. One of us should have.

Martinez started to head across the street as I dialed. With luck, he'd bump into the woman, and she'd be eating instead of spending her ten dollars on drink.

CHAPTER 12

I drove us to the police station so Martinez could eat, and then left him behind in the car while I went in to see the body. Strong stomach or not, there are some things you get a pass on until at least an hour after eating.

The coroner introduced himself and showed me the body. Adina Howard was gray and bloated. She looked like she'd been in the water for more than a few hours, but I guessed that's what the cold could do.

She had blows to her head, trauma to her feet that looked like she'd been dragged across asphalt or gravel. Her side was the worst. Where she'd been hooked and weighed down, the skin was torn badly. Worse than that, the muscle layer was pulled back in a long flap, and I could see the hook had pushed through her ribs and come out a few inches lower. I'd never seen him do anything like this before, not in nine kills; he'd never gone this deep or done this kind of damage when it didn't involve taking blood. This fish wasn't going to pull away, but he'd made more than sure.

The coroner pointed at the tear made around one of the holes. "From this lateral cutting, I gather she was alive when this happened. She started to thrash, either while he was doing it or once she was in the water. No doubt it caused quite a lot of pain."

Her left temple had been crushed in from a blow bad enough to put her out for a few hours, at least. It was likely she'd only come back to consciousness when she felt the cold water. But the shape of the trauma to her skull looked different from what I usually saw. Deeper. More like what a hammer would do. Whatever he'd used before had stayed on the surface—it was flat and not sharp, spread the contact across a few inches. This left a smaller hole.

The coroner led me to a table with a metal pan in it that held the treble hook he'd removed. He'd clipped off one of its barbs to get it out, and I could see the two full barbs and where the other stopped. The clipped barb lay next to the hook in the pan.

"I had to cut this off to get a good look at the hole."

"What's a hook this big usually used for catching?"

"Most anything up here," he said. "If you fish off a boat, or even if you're down at the Fishing Hole, halibut. Even salmon, if you wanted to snag."

Each of the three barbs looked about the length of a finger.

"I've only seen this once before," the coroner said. He didn't have any other bodies in the room, just this woman on her gurney, and I could tell he had a mind to talk. I didn't answer, just took out my pad and got ready to listen.

He told me about the case from summer of 2006, when Tina Bruce had similarly been left out on the Spit. I'd been here then, too, but he didn't seem to remember me. I let him keep going, willing to see what he had to say, in case any of it jarred something loose.

"But back then, the work was different. Done with a cleaner hand." He pointed at her side. "None of this tearing that you see here."

"I agree."

He stared at me, squinting his already thin eyes. "How did you—"

"I was here. On that case as well."

"Oh." He stepped back. "Yes. Maybe I remember you now. But what stuck with me about that body was the barbed wire. I'd never seen it used to restrain a person like that, not how he bound her wrists with it."

"Not here." I pointed to Howard's wrists, clear and unharmed.

"No. And Ms. Bruce's body was found off the Spit, not in the Fishing Hole. Frankly, I'm surprised anyone could find a time to go near the hole without being seen. There's *always* someone out there."

"Day and night. And still no witnesses."

He tapped his fingers together, almost as if clapping. "Strange things here. Strange things."

I got together with Martinez in the station after I was done with the coroner. He'd been taking statements from the cops who made the scene. I thanked him, and checked my e-mail to see if Linstrom's file had come through. It had, and on the department's old printer it took almost twenty minutes to print out.

By that time it was close to four, and I was getting tired so I didn't protest when Martinez pulled me aside and said we should get situated at a hotel if we were planning to spend the night. The local chief or sheriff—he seemed to wear both badges and all hats—suggested a small inn on the east end of town, far enough from tourists and cruise passengers. Martinez drove us over, explaining that he always got especially tired after a long drive and if he had a short nap he'd be ready to get back to it around dinnertime.

"Since it's still light until eleven, maybe midnight, we don't have to worry so much about making the most of the day. Might even be good to see the Spit at night. I mean, hole."

I agreed.

Our killer was out there, but he wasn't just going to fall into our laps if we cruised the streets. Most of my solved cases in San Francisco had come from stewing in the juices of the evidence, putting the pieces together slowly. Sometimes it all congealed while I was running or taking a shower. That one critical bit of information had a tendency to hide and reveal itself only out of my peripheral vision.

So I followed his suggestion and let Martinez check us in. He put his card down to charge our rooms to the Alaska office, and I didn't complain.

In my room, I stripped down to my underwear and bra. Since we hadn't stopped at the Marriott before heading down here, I had to keep the pantsuit looking good, even if I was nine-tenths of the way to finding a pair of jeans at a local store and changing into those. It was the idea of squeezing into a pair of Levi's 501s or some Wranglers that kept me from going.

As I flipped through the printout of the Sheila Wells file, I slipped back into the feeling I'd had when I noticed Samantha Parker's apartment mirrored mine and saw my name written in blood on her wall. I wasn't going to quit this case or let anyone pull me off it. He was out there, and I would find him. I'd do it my own way and in my own time, letting the clues come together as they would.

I wanted to look at the Wells file in part because I hoped that with more experience I'd have a new perspective on the evidence. Sometimes it was like that: even if I worked a case myself soup to nuts, if I went away from it for a while and then came back, it became a whole new set of facts.

This was the first case from my time in Alaska that I had a chance to read again. Now, looking through it, everything seemed so rudimentary, written exactly as I'd been shown in the academy by instructor Calcagno. My sentences were short and declarative, clipped like I wanted to keep out anything that might not fit. Back then, if it could be viewed as questionable, I cut it. The facts were there on the page, but little else—little sense of any theories or suspicions.

Sure, not *all* my hunches went into my reports now, but there were suggestions of where things might lead. I wondered whether, if I read through all the other files from the Daylight Case, I'd see a progression in my work.

I thought of it as the Daylight Case now, given it a name without all the difficulty. Maybe now I saw it as just another case; this perp, even if he knew my name, was just another perp in a succession of criminals out there who needed dealing with. It was still my first case, but now it wasn't my only.

Whatever I was looking for in Sheila Wells's file, I didn't find it. She'd been picked up late at night at a park where a lot of questionable people hung out. Sure enough, it'd been light out when she disappeared. My notes included the fact that the sun had set at 11:58 that night.

What more did I want? What reminded me of my mother still remained—the strange connection between her and this other woman whose life went wrong—but I couldn't see any new links to Samantha Parker. I tried to find something about Wells's father or her ex-husband, but we didn't have much. Nothing that spoke to me about the case, anyway, or told me more about why my own father had turned into a complete alcoholic prick.

I turned to the file on Adina Howard.

She was from Homer, but had last lived in Fairfax. She left Wednesday night to go home and visit her folks but never showed up. Her friends said she was planning to get a ride at least to Denali but then she'd probably hitch from there. Not too many folks thought twice about hitchhiking in Alaska, and the local authorities didn't seem to care. By the numbers, I knew the chances of something bad happening were minute—inside a couple percent. But then, every once in a while, something like this happened, and women stopped hitching alone for a few weeks or even a month. Soon enough after that, they started up again.

I hadn't had a chance to look at the day's *Anchorage Daily News* yet, but my guess was that Samantha Parker's murder was all over the front page. With this added to the mix, hitching would be quiet within the week. That wouldn't do anything for Adina Howard, though.

CHAPTER 13

When Martinez knocked on my door, it was after nine o'clock, and I'd barely napped. Out the window it was still as light as if it were noon. We agreed on hamburgers for dinner, which he went out to get. That was fine with me; they've always been a favorite.

In San Francisco, there'd be a long detailed explanation at any restaurant about where the beef was raised, how it was fed and slaughtered, organic or local or neither, but in Alaska you got none of it. And yet these were probably "greener"—grass fed and more traditionally handled than any burger in California. Or maybe they were just frozen patties from Costco. No one cared. I didn't make an issue.

"Smells good," Martinez said when he came back carrying two white paper bags. As he unwrapped a burger, I thought about explaining my California theories but saved him the aggravation.

"Ketchup?" he asked, handing me a bag full of packets.

I shook my head as I unwrapped my turkey burger deluxe. I know I'm kidding myself to think turkeys are raised any better than cows, but at least they're healthier for my arteries, supposedly. I started digging in.

While I ate, I checked my phone for voice messages and found out the brass and Special Agent Talbot wanted to know when I was going to call Senator Parker to make myself available.

"Fuck Talbot," I said, hanging up. Martinez kept eating. "How long's he been in charge up here?"

"Less than six months." Martinez avoided my eyes. If I was going to start chopping into his boss, he was wise to steer clear. Perhaps Martinez's instincts weren't so bad for a new agent after all.

"You know, the way they're kissing Senator Parker's ass is bullshit."

He shrugged. "Maybe. Or maybe you're just pissed off that we missed the plane."

I thought that over for a while as I finished eating. Martinez didn't know how little I liked heights or small planes; it wasn't something I shared.

I took the personal photos one by one from the Samantha Parker file and showed them to Martinez. In every one, we looked carefully at the men and made sure we could account for their relationship to the victim.

"You see anyone in these you think could've done this?"

"Shit, yeah." Martinez nodded, still chewing. "I'm from Ohio and hunted as a kid, but these folks up here kill bears and eat them. I don't know *what* they'd do."

"How long you been up here?"

"Eight months."

I'd been here just a year when I left. The Anchorage assignment wasn't for many of us, and once we had enough time in we usually got reassigned, moved back down to the Lower 48 to a world we understood.

"You like it?"

He looked away for a minute, toward the window and the bright sky, and then back at me. "I do, but I'm not sure how long I'll stay. I mean, it's amazing, unlike any other place I've ever been. So big and so beautiful."

He paused.

"But?"

"But I don't know. How can I say I'll stay here when I barely made it through this winter and swore I'd never stay for another? I wish I could say I'd like to live here for a while, but the truth is I have no idea. Basically Anchorage sucks."

"How about the other agents. You like the people?"

"I do. Most of 'em." He ate the last of his fries. "People up here are straight shooters. Even with an agent they're less bullshit than most folks down there." He pointed vaguely south. "But still. It's just a whole different world."

"I know what you mean."

I stood up and started stretching. "We should go cruise the Spit," I said, and that decided it.

CHAPTER 14

We drove all the way down the Spit, from where it first started, its sides littered with rough campsites and broken-down boats converted into simple houses, to where the shops, restaurants, main docks, and harbor slips began. Then past the tour offices, the Fishing Hole, the Salty Dog bar, and out to the big, fancy hotel at the very tip.

Then we turned around. "Let's try the bar," I said. "See what we can find out."

Martinez parked, and I looked over at the Salty Dog for a minute before we got out and went in. It was a working lighthouse *and* a bar, something they boasted about in the tourist literature. Our reports said it mainly served visitors these days, but a few of the fishermen came in late at night when they wanted a drink more than they cared about the company. It was also the only place for campers on the Spit to drink. Since this was a Friday night, it was busy as hell inside, and I wished Martinez and I had changed clothes, but of course neither of us had brought anything different. He'd left his suit jacket and tie in the car, but we still looked like salespeople or agents, too serious and out of place among the drinkers.

We both had to crouch below the exposed roof beams. Everything above shoulder level was covered with dollar bills stapled into the walls and ceiling beams, even taped to the lights. The dollars were signed, scrawled all over, or covered with dirty jokes. But the effect was you couldn't tell where the beams began and the dollars ended. I didn't want to hit anything with my head. It made sense that all the waitresses were short, but I wasn't. Never would be.

Two small box-TV sets showed the replay of a baseball game from earlier in the day. It had been a long time since I'd been in a bar that didn't have flat-screen HD televisions. There was something reassuring about the old box sets with cathode ray tubes that I liked. Maybe it'd lead to people being honest, as Martinez had said.

I told him I'd get us a couple of beers—he looked skeptical at first, but then nodded—and sent him off to start talking to people, asking them if they'd seen anything.

"Anyone who seems cooperative," I told him, "you buy that person a drink."

I lingered at the bar, looking at a mug shot of Steve McQueen up on the wall.

"He got arrested in Anchorage," a man said. I turned to see a hat that advertised Tecate and a beard you could comb with a fork. I caught a smell that was all sea and fish guts, something they should have made him wash off at the door. "Sorry about that," he said. "King crab slaughter today."

He told me about the king crab run and how they had him stand holding the crabs' bodies, pushing them into a sharp ax corner with a thick rubber chest protector strapped to his front. He demonstrated holding legs in each hand and leaning into the splitter, and then how the crabs came apart. "Just guts all over you," he said.

"So I smell."

"Yeah, well." He took a sip from a can of Bud and then tipped up his lowball and polished off the remains to chase it.

When the bartender came over, I ordered two drafts and re-upped what my friend was drinking.

"Obliged," he said, as he clinked his glass against mine. "Why don't you loosen up? Relax. What you doing in here dressed like this?"

"Looking for answers."

"Uh-oh."

As soon as I mentioned the girl who'd been found in the Fishing Hole, he nodded like he'd heard about it. It would be the big news of the day in this sleepy town.

I noticed a bumper sticker above the bar that read HOMER: A SMALL DRINKING TOWN WITH A BIG FISHING PROBLEM.

"Any leads?" he asked.

"Not unless you got something to tell me."

"We heard a scream from off one of the boats down the marina last night." He pointed toward where the boats were docked. "Going out this morning early, we heard it, but didn't have the chance to stop." He shrugged, as if to ask what they could have done.

He told me it'd been about six a.m. when they went out, and had just heard the one scream of a woman while they were leaving. At that time, it was more likely to have been the woman I spoke to finding Adina Howard than her being attacked. He hadn't noticed anything out of the ordinary when he looked over at the docks—moored fishing boats mostly, and it wasn't odd to see a tourist come up in a sailboat or something and tie in for the night.

"Said they found her in the Fishing Hole," my new friend said. He gave his name as Dave Heyes and told me what boat he'd been out on—the *Crab Spot*. He took a pull of his whiskey—Tullamore Dew, it turned out, at least when I was paying—and pushed out his lower lip. "Reminds me of a few summers back when that fucker was killing all those girls 'round the state."

I let that sit for a minute and drank my beer.

Heyes lit a cigarette, and I watched its cherry burn as he sucked down the smoke. Even here in Alaska, most of the bars were non-smoking now. But not the Salty Dog.

Martinez stopped by to pick up his beer, and I sent him off to the pool room to see if he could find anyone else to talk to.

I noticed the bar's other door then, and a man standing next to it, wearing a baseball hat and a blue hooded sweatshirt. He seemed to be looking in my direction. He gave me a strange nod.

I tried to get more out of Heyes for five or ten minutes, but other than thoughts about Homer in general, its tides, and the best places to drop crab pots, he didn't have much to offer.

"Just not like someone from around here to do that," he said finally. He shook his head. "Not like what you see around here."

I thought of the views outside and the lovely stretch of water leading right up to the foot of the mountains, the peaks far above covered with snow. Maybe the landscape would take murder out of a person. Maybe not.

Through a small window, I could see it was still light out, even coming up on eleven o'clock. When I glanced at the back door again, Blue Sweatshirt still had his eyes on me like he had something to say—pickup, come-on, or just wanting to know who the fuck I was to wear business clothes in a place like this. I decided it was time to find out.

With a clink of Heyes's glass, I left him at the bar to stew in his Tullamore. Blue Sweatshirt eyed me all the way across the room as I came toward him. He smoked a cigarette now and was drinking whiskey straight with a can of Blue Ribbon. I looked toward the back room and the pool table, and saw Martinez talking to two guys in trucker hats. One wore a down vest. They were pointing and talking, and Martinez looked as if he was interested in what they had to say.

I took out my wallet as I walked over and got ready to show my badge. "How things going over here tonight?" I asked. "Want to tell me what all's going on?"

His eyes never left mine.

"This you?" He lifted his right hand and pointed to a dollar bill tacked into the wall alongside his head. The dollar bill had my name, *Harding*, written across it in thick black marker and under-lined twice.

"What?"

He took my right hand in both of his. "Got something for you," he said.

Then I saw a flash of silver and felt a searing pain rip across my palm. I closed my eyes for a second, and when I opened them again, he was half out the back door.

My hand was full of blood.

CHAPTER 15

"Martinez!" I screamed.

I dropped my beer and pressed my left hand into my right. My thumb brushed against the open flaps of skin on my palm, and for a moment I felt faint. The beer glass had crashed on the floor, and all of a sudden everyone was quiet.

"Martinez."

I started to fall and he caught me. "What?"

"My hand. I—"

A waitress was there, pushing a rag into my hand and for only a second I cared if it was clean.

Then I snapped back into the world—one full of people, sounds, and colors.

"What happened? Who did this?" Martinez asked as I regained control of my legs.

"There!" I pointed to the back door and pushed myself off Martinez to go after the guy, doing my best to keep moving, clenching the rag in my hand.

As I broke through the back door, I hobbled and ran around to the front of the bar to see the street in both directions. In the distance, toward the tip of the Spit, I saw a person silhouetted against the gray light of the sky. I spun fast, back toward the docks, and saw Martinez. I realized my guy could have gone that way, too, taken off for a boat to drive across the water or just hidden somewhere in a hull.

"Go that way." I pointed toward the docks. "A blue sweatshirt and a red hat! That's our guy."

Martinez took another step in my direction, bless his heart, and I pointed him away. "Go!" He went, and I spun back to the road, running toward the person I'd seen in the distance.

As I passed by the front of the bar, I saw Heyes standing outside. When he saw me running, he put his head down and started to puff alongside. I wasn't sure how far he'd make it, but I was glad to see his effort.

Being a woman in the FBI means you have to find a good cross between a pair of dress shoes and track shoes for the times you have to run. Sure, we all work out, but when you see an actress on TV running all over a city in heels, it's bullshit; in real life our feet bleed if we do that. Over the years, I'd found a pair of flats that looked decent but also allowed me to run without great pain. I hoped Martinez wore shoes he'd be able to keep up in.

I ran the best I could, knowing a fast first burst could get me close enough to the person I'd seen to know if it was him. Up ahead I saw a sort of gazebo at the end of a parking lot, and then I saw *him* break out from between two cars—Blue Fucking Sweatshirt. He saw me and started running faster, heading away from the bar.

"Shit." I ran for a few minutes but then slowed to a jog, pacing myself. He was heading for the closed end of the Spit, and I'd catch up to him eventually if I could keep him in sight. I'd need to have something left in the tank for when I did.

I glanced down at the rag in my hand and saw it was now totally red with blood. If it'd been dry and clean before or wet and full of germs didn't matter—I was fully committed. With my left hand, I reached around to my lower back and pulled my weapon, the smallish Glock 23 that I liked because it didn't make a big outline in my clothes. Still had plenty of .40-cal kick and a thirteen-round magazine plus one in the chamber to keep me backed up. Another thing I liked about this gun was the LaserMax sight attached right below the barrel, a feature that'd kept me from firing a single round over the years. Somebody catches sight of a red dot on his chest, he's quick to put up his hands.

I wasn't the best at shooting with my off hand, but I'd trained with it enough that I could make do. Not one-handed or on the run, maybe, but that shit only works on TV.

When I looked back, I saw Heyes already fading. At least he'd been good to try.

I checked for cars and crossed the street at an angle, hoping to get a better view of my runner if he made any change in direction. Sure enough, he cut down away from the road after the gazebo, heading for the beach. What I saw there was a lot of trucks parked together in rows, and I knew that was going to be trouble. This guy wouldn't just run to nothing. He'd hide in the back of a truck or up and drive away. Lot of good fourteen .40-caliber rounds would do trying to shoot out the tires on an eighteen-wheeler.

Across the street from the gazebo—an elaborate construction around a big metal bell, I could see now—I slowed up. I couldn't hear anyone's feet pounding gravel or pavement. Heyes was too far behind, and no one else made a sound. Out this far on the Spit at this hour, there was no traffic, not even boats. Then I heard the engine of a big truck starting.

I took one quick look back and saw Heyes still chugging. He had another guy with him from the bar now, a tall man who ran uneasily. Halfway up the row of trucks, I saw the twin exhausts of a white Mack cab kicking out fumes, its caps popping. But the truck hadn't moved. I crossed the street and walked sideways across the front of the cabs to see if I could get there before he drove out. The white Mack was the only one making noise.

"Come on," I said. I pressed my hands around the gun and felt the squeeze of the wet rag, a jolt through my arm from the pain in my hand. I stepped back to have a shot at the windshield if I needed it. The red dot of my LaserMax popped over the grilles of the first few trucks, tracking across to the one that was live. I considered taking a shot preemptively, hoping to slow it, but I still didn't even know if my man was inside.

At the white Mack, I crept up to the cab and pulled myself onto the running panel using my right hand. Another shot of pain. It hurt, but I wasn't going to take the gun out of my left. I couldn't see anything through the little window along the lower half of the door, so I poked my hand up and knocked on the glass with the barrel of my gun.

"What? Who is it?" came from inside.

"Turn off the engine and exit the vehicle with your hands up." I tapped the glass again with my gun in case the driver hadn't seen it.

"Whoa!" a surprised voice called from inside. I knew something was wrong.

CHAPTER 16

Heyes showed up at the front of the cab, and I waved him around to the driver's side, hoping he wouldn't regret it.

A voice said, "Okay. I'm coming out."

Now I looked up through the window and saw a gray-bearded trucker holding his hands up and opening the cab's other door. He wore a white sweatshirt. I wanted to swear, but I pursed my lips instead and breathed hard through my nose. The trucker moved away from me, toward Heyes, but his eyes still watched my gun. The red dot on his chest had that effect.

I took my finger off the trigger and switched off the laser. The red dot disappeared. The trucker shuddered and released a sigh I could see. "Take it easy, old-timer," I said through the glass. I held my gun up, pointing the barrel at the sky.

"Here, let me help." The other guy from the bar was behind me, offering to help me down from the truck's door. He took my elbow, and I let him ease me back to the ground. He had a beard and he was tall. Hearing his wheezing and Heyes hacking on the other side of the truck, I felt good for a moment about my own conditioning. The early morning runs had paid off. But that was part of my job.

I came around to find Heyes and the old trucker standing together. The trucker wasn't my guy, and he wasn't wheezing either—he hadn't just run *anywhere*. Instead he looked like he just woke up.

I swore under my breath. "Did you see anyone else out here? Guy wearing a hat and a blue sweatshirt?"

To my surprise, the trucker nodded. "Yeah. I just saw a guy get into that cab over there."

All four of us jerked around to look at the next truck, what looked like a dark gray, slightly smaller sleeper cab model of the white Mack.

I stepped back and raised my gun again, finger on the trigger, and flicked on the laser. The red dot popped up on the passenger door. I nodded the others back from the cab, and they stepped away fast. At the far end of the truck, I saw a quick movement, and then it was gone before I'd shifted my gun in its direction.

"Harding, it's me!" Martinez showed his badge and gun extended in front of him as he came around the end of the truck. His shoulders were pumping up and down from the run, but his gun kept steady.

I tipped my head at its cab, and Martinez nodded, slipped around back to circle his way to the driver's side.

"We've got you surrounded in there," I said. I didn't want to step up onto the door for what the effort had done to my hand the last time—it still throbbed and I had no doubt I was losing more blood. The windshield of the cab was black; I couldn't see anyone inside.

"He in there," Heyes said from behind me. The old-timer said something, too, but I couldn't make it out.

Then Martinez was at the driver's door, pulling himself up to look inside. He tapped the window with his gun.

"I have you covered," I said.

Martinez knocked on the window again. "You want to come out, or we coming in?"

I played the red dot of the laser across the windshield in no particular pattern, hoping that if my guy was inside, he'd see the beam and know more about what he was dealing with.

"This is the FBI. Go ahead and open the door for my partner *now*!"

Martinez tapped at the window, and we all waited. After a handful of breaths, a voice answered from inside. "I'm coming out," it said. "Don't want no trouble."

"Show us your hands!"

"I'm showing! I'm showing!"

Martinez nodded from the step-up and told our guy to unlock the door. He swung back to make room for it to open. "Come on out now."

I kept my gun on the door as it opened, and then I saw him: the guy from the bar. I knew it was him even without his hat. My hand stung just to look at him.

"Fuck *me*."

As he stepped out, Martinez hit him in the back and threw him down. I came around the front of the truck and saw his blue sweatshirt. The guy was down on one knee, struggling to get up.

"That's him," the old-timer said.

Martinez pulled the guy up and pushed him over to me; his hands were cuffed behind him, and he stumbled uncomfortably.

"You fuck," I said. My right hand pulsed. I wanted to punch him in the face with it. I had to use my left. I let the gun spin in my hand so the butt stuck out from my palm, and used it to slap him across the cheek.

Martinez caught him. The guy coughed and spit blood onto the ground. I wanted to see a tooth or two in the mix. Heyes said, "I didn't see that."

"*Fucker!*" I'd never been hurt in the field before, which made the pain worse; I knew I'd be seeing this guy in my mind's eye for years to come as I looked at my hand and its scar. I kicked him in his shoulder.

Martinez dropped the knife on the ground in front of me—a short-bladed hunting knife that said *Alaska* along the handle and had a picture of a salmon jumping out of a stream. I cursed him again. Then something strange happened: in a second I realized it felt off, him being our guy for the murders. This wasn't our Daylight

Killer. I didn't feel the fear I had before; I didn't feel anything about him but mad.

I could see he was just a person, not the monster I knew I had to find.

Even now, after all the events of the day, the sky was no darker than a light gray. The sun might have gone down below the horizon, but the sky seemed to have its own light that would go on forever.

Heyes coughed and hacked.

I looked around for the other guy who'd been running with us, but now no one else was there. "Where's that other guy?" I asked.

Martinez said, "You did this to these women? You fuck!" He kicked Blue Sweatshirt in the back, against the side of the truck.

"It's not our guy," I said, but not loud enough for anyone else to hear.

Martinez kicked him again. "Who are you?"

"Jason Andrews," he said. "Wait. This is all a mistake."

"Fuck it is. You just cut my partner's hand open with a knife, jackass. That's assault on a federal agent."

"I—I mean, he…*He* paid me to do it. How did I know who you were?"

Martinez said, "You fucking look at us, dumbass. We look like fishermen to you?"

"Who paid you?" I said.

"That guy." Blue Sweatshirt pointed with his chin, but now Heyes was standing where the other guy had been. "Who was that guy, anyway?"

"Wait. What?" I turned around. A siren called in the distance, the local cops finally racing to the scene, but I didn't see anyone.

Andrews moved his head like a nervous chicken, darting his gaze all around in quick twitches. "He was just here. I thought you knew him. That guy—he paid me four hundred bucks to call you

Harding and mark your hand. Shit. I mean, that's *four hundred bucks.*"

"He was here? *Him?*" Martinez asked.

"Shit." I rushed to the end of the trucks, but suddenly my legs felt weak.

Heyes was next to me. "You all right?"

"Yeah." I pushed myself to the street and looked back. No one was between us and the Salty Dog. A crowd had gathered in front of the bar around a police car, its lights whirling.

"He was just here," I said. I had to lean against the back of a truck to stay up.

I heard Andrews behind me. "I swear I didn't know!"

Then Martinez, "Assault, motherfucker! How stupid are you?"

Heyes said, "You don't look too good. You okay?"

I swore. "Get the car. I think I need a hospital."

Someone said, "I'm on it." It was the last thing I heard before I blacked out.

CHAPTER 17

Turns out the closest hospital wasn't even a mile north. It took us less than five minutes to get there, and even without FBI status or a call ahead from the police, I'd have been first in line. There was that little going on.

As soon as I hit a bed, the nurse gave me a shot of something that made everything go soft.

She said, "This woman's lost a significant amount of blood."

People were speaking all around me, but I couldn't make out all of the words.

"Did you get the dollar?"

"What?"

"Martinez," I said. "Tell Martinez to go back and get the dollar."

Then I saw his face. He said something, but I was starting to go under.

"The dollar," I said. "Get the dollar that says Harding."

CHAPTER 18

When I looked around again, I was in a different room, a quiet single with white walls.

Martinez said, "Good to see you're up."

I laughed, struggling onto my elbows with effort. "Can't keep a good woman down."

Then I felt dizzy.

"They said you lost some blood but would be fine in a couple hours. Gave you enough painkillers to knock you out for the night."

"How many stitches?" I let myself down onto my back again.

He shook his head. "You'll have to ask the doc."

Out the window, I saw sky light blue and pale, almost white closer to the horizon. I pushed myself up.

"What time is it?"

"Morning. About nine o'clock and you already missed coffee." He held up a paper cup and shook it. Empty.

"Shit. We're wasting time." I slipped my legs out of the bed and dropped my feet to the floor. All of a sudden I wanted to throw up.

"Go slow now," Martinez said. "I'll call the nurse."

"Shit." I ran my hand over my face. Greasy hair hung around my cheeks. I must have looked like shit. I tried wiggling my toes, felt the funny hospital socks with the rubber treads on the bottom. The only other things I had on were underwear and a gown. I wanted badly to lie back down.

"I just need a shower. Where's the shower?"

"Relax, Harding. You had a rough night."

"We have to go. He's close."

I exhaled hard and looked up. Martinez held his hands out to show I shouldn't rush.

"Do we know where he is?"

"Who?"

I made a face, and suddenly Martinez looked like he wanted to apologize.

"We got Andrews in custody, but not the dollar bill with your name on it. If someone else paid him, we couldn't find that guy anywhere."

"You talking to the other people in the bar?"

"Locals, we got their names, and the police are putting together their statements. I spent a few hours going at Andrews last night, but he's an empty vessel. Fucking loser just met our man and picked up a buck, he says. Had no freaking idea who you were."

I held the side of the bed with both hands. "I'm going at him today. Where is he?"

"At the jail. They're holding him." Martinez paused. "Got good and bad from Anchorage. You want it?"

I focused on my breathing. The gauzy feeling around my head and the tightening in my chest were starting to ease. "Give me the good."

"They're concerned about you. Talbot authorized a sketch artist to put together a composite profile from witnesses. We get enough of a face to go on and maybe we have something to lead a search with."

"Bad?"

"They want you back up there to make nice for Senator Parker and to talk through what happened last night. They want a Bureau doctor to look you over."

"Pass me my pants." I pointed at the hanger in the closet. He passed me the whole thing. I looked over the pantsuit I was supposed to be taking care of. The jacket had scuffs on the sleeves from where I'd gone down in the dirt. The pants weren't much better: any crease was long gone and the knees showed dirt, too. I tried brushing it off.

"Guess I'll need to go up there for a change of clothes, anyway." I sucked air, trying to get up the strength to slip into my pants. "Where's breakfast?"

"That's the spirit, now. I'll get the nurse."

I checked my hand and realized I could still make a half fist. "At least turn around."

He got up. "Better yet, I'll go find you some food and coffee. We good?"

I nodded. Sure, my clothes were a mess, my hand was cut open, and I felt like I'd just eaten a cabinet of sleeping pills. I also needed a shower, badly. All was definitely going my way. "Tell Talbot to send the fucking plane."

He left, and I got myself onto two feet and into the small bathroom across from the bed. Luckily it had handles along the wall and in the shower. I needed them all as I got myself under the spray, holding my bandaged hand as high as I could so it wouldn't get wet. I ducked my head into the water, waiting for it to wake me up. Someone's voice inside my head said to go back to bed and sleep it off, to use the damned sick time and get paid for my troubles. But that felt like what my father would do—maybe it was even his voice that had said it. A burst of guilt in my chest got me upright. My father would milk this for all it was worth, forget the case, and just take it easy. That wasn't me.

I turned the water a little colder, let it wash in and out of my mouth, found some soap and washed my face and hair the best I could with one hand.

Soon I started feeling like myself again.

Back in my room, Martinez stood with a worried-looking nurse who held my breakfast tray. "Ms. Harding," she said. "Are you sure you're up to this?"

I had a sudden instinct to correct her, to let her know I was "Agent Harding," but I let it slide. Better for relations.

"Going to have to work on this case today, I'm afraid. No time to be hurt."

Martinez said, "We have a witness to interview, and then we're wanted back in Anchorage." The look on his face was conflicted, as if he wanted to support me but really agreed with the nurse. I wondered how bad I really looked.

"Forms," I said. "You know how that is."

She set the tray down on a bedside table and took my bad hand in both of hers, checking to be sure it was dry. Somewhere inside there I had stitches or staples. I didn't know which or how many, and I wasn't sure I wanted to. Just the fact that I could move my fingers was gift enough.

Martinez said, "I'll call Linstrom, see if he can put them off."

The nurse seemed to like what she felt—at least enough to let me go with a few instructions and a stern warning. Stitches, it turned out. Twelve of them.

I looked under the lid of the breakfast plate: bacon and eggs. I gulped coffee and forked the food into a paper cup to take to go.

CHAPTER 19

If our man was in Homer, or had been, then he had less than a twelve-hour head start. I was finally getting somewhere, even if I'd needed a trip to the hospital to recover. My clothes were a wreck, I wore no makeup, and I hadn't been able to blow-dry my hair, but I felt a certain rush being on his tail.

It's the adrenaline from progress in a case that drives so many of us, like the thrill of good competition in a sport, and I'm no different. I wanted this guy—to crush him and bring him to justice. He was testing me, testing my intelligence and what I could do as an agent. He was going to get so much more than I'd offered in 2006. He was about to get my all.

I wanted to go at Andrews alone, press him for whatever we could get. Like a bug on the path to my larger goal, he would fall and get squashed along the way. I clenched my good hand in the car to the station, eager to take him down. This was the second person in two days who'd actually seen our suspect—two more witnesses than I'd ever gotten in 2006. If he was right, I'd even seen the guy myself. *He touched me!* I felt the spot on my elbow where he'd helped me down from the side of the truck. I wanted to feel some odd burn but didn't.

"Fuck me!"

Martinez asked, "What?" but didn't slow the car. He must have been getting used to me.

I told Martinez I wanted to go at Andrews alone and what to say if the local law didn't let me have my shot. He'd come in and stay quiet, stand in the corner looming like he'd rip off our boy's ears if he said anything wrong.

Sure enough, the sheriff didn't want me alone with Andrews. Closed-circuit camera, two-way mirror, and people in the next room, and he still didn't want him in there with just me. I couldn't tell whether this was to protect me from him or him from me. Probably the second.

I chose Martinez over an Alaskan in a uniform. We went into a holding box where they had Andrews sitting cuffed to a table. His sweatshirt was gone for prison orange, and his hair looked like he'd want his hat back to cover it up.

"Nice bald spot," I said, coming around the table to sit down. Martinez hovered along the wall, making himself known and leaning in and out of Andrews's peripheral vision.

I sat down. "We do this easy or hard," I said. Martinez stepped in and put his hands on the table. "He's in here to protect you from the hard. For now."

"I already talked to *him*." Andrews looked at Martinez. He hadn't slept and wasn't going to, which I liked. He reached out his hands to me, not to apologize or ask for mercy, but like I was supposed to help him. Basically, he acted like the piece of shit he was.

My leg pulsed under the table, knee bouncing like a junkie's.

"I told you, I only did it for the money. Thought that dude was just mad at an old girlfriend and wanted to get back at her. I mean, that wasn't the nicest thing I done. I ain't proud. But it ain't the worst thing neither."

"Fuck you," I said. "That's first. Second is shut the fuck up."

He pulled back like this surprised him.

"We good?"

He nodded.

I looked over my file on Andrews: He lived in Juneau, worked fishing boats, moved around, and occasionally drove a shipment for Walmart up from Salt Lake City. Part-time trucker, part-time fisherman, full-time opportunist.

"How much you make doing that run from Salt Lake?"

"Take me four days to make eight hundred dollars. And that's a lot of miles."

"Bet it does something to a man's head, being alone on the road for long stretches of time like that. Just you and the highway."

"Like I said, lady. It's a lot of miles."

I looked him over, trying to figure my best tack. He could use a cigarette, that was clear, and I produced a pack from my briefcase that I kept for occasions such as these. It was a box of Marlboros—Reds—and when I set it on the table, his expression shifted.

"We talk like civilized people here, and you get the smoke I can see you need. You whine or fuck around, I make sure you don't get out of Homer until thaw."

He nodded, and something loosened in his eyes. I saw his glance pause on my hand and then dart away. The bandage wrapped up to my wrist. In the car I had two weeks' worth of antibiotics and Extra-Strength Tylenol for the pain. So far, I'd taken neither, and a dull ache came from my palm. But I could feel blood pumping in it to tell me I was alive.

"Twelve stitches and I was in the hospital for the night. You think about that when you took the money?"

He shook his head. I watched his eyes go from me, to the cigarettes, to my hand, and back to his hands.

"What you want to know?"

"You didn't know this guy at all?"

He shook his head.

"Never seen him?"

"No."

"So a stranger at a bar offers you four hundred bucks to commit assault on a woman and you *agree* to this?" I pulled back to eye him in full. "What kind of a fucking wing nut are you?"

"I—It's a lot of money," he said.

I turned to Martinez. "You believe this guy? Who *does* some shit like that?"

Martinez said, "I couldn't tell you. Must be somebody really fucked up. Maybe we should just ice his ass for a few months in the biggest prison we can find."

"Give him a cellmate who likes little white guys."

Andrews blanched a bit at this thought. I leaned closer.

"Let me tell you about this guy you met. We make him for killing nine women now, all of them more deserving of life and anal virginity than you are. Maybe you've read about him in the papers or seen something on TV. Five years ago, this was a big case. Then it went away. Now it's back."

Some recognition passed in his eyes.

"With me?"

He nodded carefully.

"You're our first witness who talked to him, put him at a scene, saw his face, and heard what he sounds like. Get me?"

"You saw him, too. He was—"

"I want everything you can tell me. Any detail, whether it seems big or small to you, could mean something. Maybe it helps us place him somewhere else, track a lead, find out who he is." I opened the pack so he could see the rows of cigarettes inside and their brown filters. "You give me nothing, your ass goes to Herm the Human Wrecker."

I let him have one last look at the cigarettes and then I closed the pack. "So I want everything you can give. Get me?"

"A tattoo," Andrews said. "Guy had a tat on the top of his hand by his thumb. Some kind of weird word in another language. You know?"

"Like what? Tell me more."

"Like the Kremlin or something. Like Gorbachev kind of writing. Backwards letters."

"Cyrillic." Martinez started making notes on a pad.

"Our boy's a fucking genius, eh, René? Gorbachev, he says."

Martinez looked hurt that I'd used his first name, especially in front of a witness. I'd apologize later. Truth was, I was pretty keyed up that a tattoo on our guy's hand matched some of the strange writing I'd seen in blood on victims' walls.

I noticed a few tattoos on Andrews's own hands and arms. "How old was he?"

"My age. Mid-thirties or something. I'm thirty-four."

I nodded, waiting.

"Weird thing, though." He turned over his right hand to show me his palm where I now had a gash thanks to his pocketknife. He traced the line of the cut, just like where he'd sliced me. "He had a cut here on his palm. Like he asked me to give you."

"Like you *gave* her." Martinez slapped the back of Andrews's head. Andrews opened his mouth to complain, but I cut him off.

"You don't want to *think* about complaining to me."

Andrews used his nail to mime cutting along his palm. "He showed me on his hand what he wanted you to have. His cut, you know? He wanted me to give you the same thing."

"And you didn't ask him why?" I couldn't believe the stupidity of this one. "Or tell him to fuck off?"

"He said you two shared something in common, your careers or something. He said he wanted you to have his mark."

Something chilled inside me, and fresh pain shot through my hand.

Martinez stood up off the wall and leaned on the table next to Andrews. "Tell us more," he said.

"Those were his hands. He had some ink on his neck, too." He touched the space between his ear and the neckline of his shirt. "On one side it was some more of those words. Not so big," he said. "What'd you call them?"

"Cyrillic, asshole."

"Yeah, that." He didn't blink at what I'd called him, probably was used to the concept by now.

"On the other side another tat. Different. A man's face. Bearded guy."

I watched Martinez's hands on the table. He leaned over Andrews. "People love to get tattoos these days. Just like you, am I right?"

Andrews shook his head. "Not on my neck, man. Face and neck off-limits."

"No? Not the neck tattoos? I thought those were real popular with scumbags."

Andrews started to spill. He looked rattled. "It looked like Jesus. You know, Christ figure." He closed his eyes to think. "I mean with a crowd of thorns and all. That thing. Religious signs."

"*A crowd of thorns,*" I repeated. "Jesus. Tell me again about his hand. How old did this cut look?"

Andrews chewed the inside of his cheek. "Old. It was healed up but still red."

I found the *Alaska* knife in my briefcase and lifted it out by its evidence bag. I set it on the table. "Tell me about this. It yours?"

Andrews shook his head. "He give it to me. But they're cheap. You can buy them anyplace. I used to have one for fishing, but mine was bigger."

The lab had fingerprinted the knife and found only Andrews's prints on it. "How did he hand it to you?"

"Just like you would. Had it in his hand and just give it to me. Hey—" Andrews nodded at the Marlboros. "How 'bout a smoke now?"

I held the pack open and let him take one. Then lit it for him with a match. On the table was a small, silver ashtray made of cardboard. I pushed it his way. I was tempted to smoke one myself but didn't like Reds. They hurt my throat. I'd hit a point where the adrenaline was starting to wear off, the night in the hospital was catching up with me, and I felt tired. Tired and worse. My face was still dry, dirty like I had makeup caked into my eyes. I needed more coffee or something stronger: a good meal or a place to sleep.

Andrews took a long drag and leaned back. Suddenly the room stilled, and I felt sick. I realized I'd been jiggling my leg under the table the whole time. Andrews exhaled up above us, and his face loosened.

"I am sorry about what I did to you. I had a few beers. More than a few. I made a bad decision, but I'm doing the best I can now."

Martinez said, "You're going to talk to a sketch artist, give him everything you remember, and he's going to try and make a composite facial image for us."

"I can do, you let me have a few more of those." He nodded toward the Marlboros.

I was wondering how there weren't any other fingerprints on the knife. "Did he wear gloves?"

Andrews squinted like he was thinking, but then he shook his head. "Gloves? No, ma'am."

Then Martinez took off his jacket and rolled up his shirtsleeve to the elbow. On the inside of his forearm, he had a tattoo of Jesus.

"This face look like the tattoo you saw?"

"Yeah," Andrews said. "That's him. Jesus."

"Take a good look now. Because you need to pray."

CHAPTER 20

We went back to the hotel to get our things, and I took a long, hot shower with soap and shampoo that was only slightly better than the hospital's. I kept my hand in a plastic bag to keep it dry. When I got out, I dressed in the new finery that I'd purchased in Homer's best hardware store. The place even sold groceries. Bless America.

All of this helped get me close to feeling half normal for the five-hour ride back upstate.

Being Saturday, all the traffic on the Sterling Highway was headed south, the opposite direction from us, so we could make good time. I closed my eyes for twenty minutes, and then I started looking at maps.

Alaska had only three roads you could consider "highways," and even these hardly ever had more than two lanes. From Homer, our guy would have only one choice for leaving, unless he was traveling by boat or plane. If he was, then we had no hope of tracking him, no way to follow his trail across water or through the sky.

East of Homer, the small local roads all ended within a few dozen miles. Beyond that was the Chugach Mountains, which go straight up to the Harding Icefield, a stretch of pure ice and snow that runs for almost fifty miles. No way our man was going through that or across it without a plane. If he did, Martinez and Linstrom had both made it clear that we—which is to say, I—did not have one in which to follow.

I called Linstrom as Martinez drove and spent ten minutes trying to talk my way out of coming in for a debrief. By a stroke of luck, Senator Parker had been called back to the Lower 48 on official business, but the special agents up from DC still wanted to see me.

I gave Linstrom everything from Adina Howard, which wasn't much: more water damage than anything else, other than the lack of barbed wire and the coroner's hunch about it being different from the murder five years ago.

He asked about my hand and clucked his tongue a few times. "Why don't you just come back to Anchorage, and we'll go have a drink and talk this over, get you a good meal. It sounds like you could use a chance to unwind."

Out the window, I saw trees and the occasional ad for fishing tours. I wasn't completely sure what he meant by "unwind," but I told him I might be ready for something like that. Martinez watched the road and tried to keep a straight face, but I could tell he was listening. I wondered if I should start asking him to put on headphones when I called in.

Linstrom had a smile in his voice when he said, "It would be my pleasure." Then I reminded him I hadn't seen Owens yet, and that stopped him cold. "Why would you want to see him?"

Martinez smiled, confirming he'd heard the rumors about me and Steve Owens, the Anchorage office evidence technician who specialized in blood work. Headphones for him were definitely a good idea.

"To talk about the scene at Samantha Parker's apartment, for one."

"But I can tell you the whole file." A note of desperation crept into his voice, and he started to spill. They'd confirmed that not all the blood at Samantha Parker's was hers. Who else it belonged to, they weren't yet sure. It wasn't Adina Howard's; she'd been killed almost twenty-four hours later.

"That's the strange thing," Linstrom said. "This could mean there's another body, but so far we don't have one."

"You have to wonder if it's his," I said. "Wouldn't put it past him, Oscar. Not this fuck."

Linstrom didn't say anything about my name on Samantha Parker's kitchen wall. That fact was *not* going to find its way into my report—not for a while, at least. Since Martinez hadn't been able to find the dollar bill with my name on it, I wasn't mentioning that bit of information either. I wanted to stay on this case as long as I could. This was *my guy*, and I was getting close. I could sense him in the air. I wanted this bust even more now that it had cost me twelve stitches.

"Oh, and that evidence you were asking about? A17? I tracked that down, too."

"And?" I got excited for a moment but also mad that someone had been holding out on me.

"It's nothing. Just a bag of coke we're pretty sure belonged to Ms. Parker. I think the brass was trying to keep it from the press, helping the senator avoid scandal."

"The fucks." But it made sense. No need to blow this into a story about a girl with a drug problem. I just wished someone had told me about it.

I didn't like how Martinez kept looking at me so I turned on the radio in the car, hoping the satellite would come through. Instead, nothing. Just a screen that read SEARCHING FOR SIGNAL. We sped on through the bright afternoon sun, and I saw a moose by the side of the road, peacefully eating leaves off a bush.

"Thanks for all this, Oscar." I tried to sound grateful but wasn't sure it came across. Linstrom was sticking his neck out for me and that meant something. I wanted him to know that I knew.

He asked where else I would go *but* Anchorage and he had a point. Until I found another scene to investigate or got a sketch back from Andrews, I had little to do but come in and cool off.

"There's nothing down in Homer for you."

"Nothing but a guy who took money from our suspect to cut my hand and then did it. I think I'm getting under the killer's skin."

"Jesus, Jess. This one's got you wrapped tight all over again."

"Not again, Oscar. Still."

"Okay, good. We're catching some breaks here; the case is developing. Come back up and we'll escalate from here, put out the full-court press. You need to slow down for a bit to let yourself heal."

"I'm coming, but you better keep those DC boys off my ass. And don't talk to me again about taking time off."

We passed a sign announcing the turnoff for Nikolaevsk, and I held up my hand for Martinez to stop. "I got to go," I told Linstrom. He tried to stop me, but I hung up.

Martinez slowed along the roadside, stopped about twenty yards beyond the turn. We both turned around to look at a sign saying Nikolaevsk was fifteen miles east.

"You really want to go down there?"

It didn't look like much of a road. Unpaved dirt ran right into the woods.

"Sure do. A few of the murders last time had words in Cyrillic on the walls, and maybe that's a tie-in to the tat Andrews saw on our man's hand. Truth is, we don't know *what's* going on up there. So I'd say it sounds weird enough to investigate, even on a hunch, even and especially if my other choice is a debrief back in Anchorage."

Martinez backed up and turned onto the dirt road.

"You know he likes you, right?"

I gave him a slight nod, hoping he'd leave it there.

"And with Owens," he said, "you know those two haven't seen eye to eye since you left?"

"Old news, Martinez. Nothing anyone wants to discuss."

That shut him up, at least for the time being.

CHAPTER 21

Outside our windows flat, green fields stretched to the horizon, broken only by tall pines and short bushes. To the far east, I could see mountains. Woods for miles before them. The land was still and the sun bright. We drove in silence.

After a time, Martinez said, "Old Believers?"

"They still mainly speak Russian. I'm hoping they'll know something about the Cyrillic tattoo. If not, at least we can warn them about our guy."

What I didn't tell him was that I really had no idea what we'd find.

"If we're lucky," I said, "we'll find something that helps our case."

A homemade sign by the road announced Nikolaevsk, without population or elevation. There was nothing else to show any difference in the terrain as we continued.

Martinez said, "Guess it's still up ahead."

We'd driven for twenty-five minutes and passed a few run-down houses, more cars left to rot in the grass than I could count. In some places, if you have enough land you'll leave a dead car out to rot, forgotten but for parts you might someday use. After a while, they litter the landscape, only noticed by newcomers who aren't blind to them. This place was one of those; the dead cars were all over.

"Thanks again for driving."

"I don't mind. This has been better than anything I've done in this office. I'm sure as shit getting to see more." His phone buzzed against his hip, and he looked down at it. He pressed a button, and it went quiet. "If we don't get back to the office by tonight, though, I'm going to see a whole storm of crap. Linstrom or not."

"I hear you. We'll check in."

I saw a few buildings come into view up ahead: long, metal barns. Technically, it was up in the air as to whether we held any federal jurisdiction over these people—they still thought of themselves as citizens of Russia and were basically recognized by Alaska as such—but I hadn't mentioned that to Martinez, and I didn't plan to. I'd already told him they were likely to carry AK-47s and considered myself lucky he'd come this far.

"Slow down." Up ahead, I saw the first building I could consider a house, and I didn't want to piss anybody off.

Three people—two women and a man—were on the front porch, looking us over. They appeared weathered but strong, as if they'd been working fields in the sun their whole lives. As we got closer, I could tell the first woman was older than the other two. She was sitting. The man wore a little hat like a Civil War soldier, crossed rifles and all. He might as well have had a wheat stalk hanging out of his mouth or been playing the theme song from *Deliverance*. Instead he spit a stream of dark tobacco juice onto his lawn.

"Should we stop?"

"Might be worth talking to them," I said. "Ask them if they know anyone who's been killing young women."

Martinez coughed at that. "Yeah. That'll go over good."

Beyond the house I saw other structures placed sparsely on either side of the road. One had a steeple with a blue onion dome, the kind that reminds you of the Kremlin or the Taj Mahal. Probably a Russian Orthodox church.

A couple of men stepped out onto the road, and Martinez stopped. They stood in front of the car, and where they'd been before that, I couldn't tell. They might have been hiding behind houses. Now they were a roadblock.

I rolled down my window and called out "hello" to the old woman on the porch. The men in front of our car didn't move.

"Jesus, Harding. What the hell *is* this?" Martinez reached inside his jacket for his gun, and I threw my hand across his arm.

"Don't."

"Sure. Then what do we do?"

"I'll get out."

"No. I wouldn't."

I opened my door and stepped out onto the road. It was paved here—they had that much going for them in the way of modernity. That and the AK-47s, which I knew were somewhere not too far out of reach.

The younger woman on the porch, who couldn't have been a day over twenty, motioned me to come closer. She said, "Tell us why you are here."

"We're looking for a man. A killer who targets young women. We want to warn you and ask if anyone has been through here."

She spoke in Russian to the older woman—translating, I hoped. The older woman responded in kind.

"Why would he come here?"

"I don't know. I just want to let you know he's dangerous, and he's out in this area." I wobbled from one foot to the other, their cold eyes fixed on every move.

The older woman turned her gaze away from me, back up the road to where we'd come from.

She spoke in Russian, and the younger woman translated. "She says you were wrong to come here. We don't know anyone who would do that."

I reached around to draw my wallet but didn't touch it. Somehow this seemed like the wrong thing to do.

The younger woman nodded toward our car. "You are federal agents of United States," she said. "We can tell this by your car."

She gave my outfit a strange look. The jeans and sweatshirt I wore, Homer Hardware's finest, didn't quite add up, even for her. "We do not need you."

Behind me, I could hear Martinez from the car. "Let's go, Harding," he said, "these people don't want to be disturbed."

I didn't want to raise the issue of jurisdiction, so I was glad he didn't push to go forward. I held up my hands. "We're just here to look around," I said. "Maybe you can help us find who we're looking for?"

The two men on the road stood tall—dark statues watching over these proceedings. I didn't have a good feeling. In truth, I really couldn't see much that'd be worth our examination or exploration. It was just some houses on an old road.

The young woman said something to the older one, who nodded. When she did, the two statues stepped away from our car, back out of the road. The younger woman came down the stairs. She held out her hand to me. "I am Alexandra."

"Harding. Jessica Harding." I reached out of the car to shake her hand with my left, keeping my bandaged right hand on the armrest. If she thought it was odd, she didn't let on.

"You are welcome to look around. But I do not think you will find much here. We live life of simple people."

I could see that was abundantly true. But I didn't want to say so and offend. After we left, I was certain they'd be sipping their afternoon tea out of little cups, through sugar cubes they held in their teeth. If I wasn't within fifty feet of a hot, waiting samovar, I'd be shocked. Still, I kept my mouth shut. These weren't the people you wanted to piss off.

"Thanks." I got back in the car next to Martinez and closed my door.

Alexandra stepped closer to my window. "Along here are our houses," she said, pointing to the next set of structures. "Beyond this our school and church. If you pass through there, you will come to our fields and the buildings where we do our harvesting and prepare our food. You have already seen some of these." She pointed back up the road.

I thanked her, and she stepped away from the car. Martinez used his controls to roll up my window, which I felt not entirely comfortable about. He started to roll forward, slowly, and said under his breath, "Let's just get the fuck out of here. Nothing for us to find and everyone for us to bother if we stick around."

As we went forward, I saw small booths on the sides of the first two houses where the road guards could have been sitting as we drove up.

"I hear you." I pointed to a driveway. "Go ahead, turn around there and we'll go back."

"Fair enough." He banked into the drive, made a quick three-point turn, and we were pointed toward the Sterling Highway. When we got to where Alexandra was still standing, he stopped and rolled down his window.

"We're good here," he said. "No need to look around after all."

I ducked to see Alexandra's face and the old woman on the porch. She hadn't moved—still sat in her chair, staring at us like she had all the time in the world.

"Well, thank you for coming, then." Alexandra shook hands with Martinez, which made him visibly uncomfortable, at least to me, and then she stepped back up the stairs. She waved at us, and Martinez started forward, driving slowly until we were a safe distance away. Then he picked up speed.

We weren't more than ten minutes down the road, less than halfway back to the highway, when Martinez said, "Uh-oh."

"What?"

He tapped the window next to his side mirror. "Look behind us."

I lowered myself in my seat to see through my side mirror. When I reached the right position, I could see what had set him off: Behind us, a motorcycle was coming up fast. It looked like one of the statue guards was driving it, helmetless, and he had Alexandra on the back—her long hair unmistakable in the breeze.

I said, "Looks like our friends have something else to tell us. Let's slow down."

"Not my first choice, but you're in charge." Martinez pulled to the side of the road and stopped. The motorcycle, really more of a dirt bike, revved loud and chugged its way up alongside us. To my right, the road dropped off into a drainage ditch, but the bike came up on my side anyway, down the slope a little. This put Alexandra's face at the same level as my own.

I had put my window down already.

She said, "I may know something about your man."

CHAPTER 22

"What?" I asked. It was all I could come up with.

She shook her head, long brown curls flopping around her shoulders. "The man who you look for." Her eyes turned down, like a kid about to confess to breaking a window. "He is one of our town. He grew up here, but he is not with us now."

To my other side, Martinez said softly, "Oh, shit."

"What's his name?"

"Now he call himself Anthony. We used call him Vitali."

I got out my notebook and wrote down both names. "We need to talk."

"Follow us to highway. There is restaurant where we can sit."

I tilted my head back toward her town. "Not back there?"

"No. *She* must not know that we talk." The guy driving the bike didn't wait for anything else. He revved the engine hard and drove off, spraying gravel against the car.

Martinez winced at the sound of rocks hitting the Town Car's side. "Shit. You know I can get charged for that?"

"Put it on my tab." I pointed up the road after the bike.

We followed them to a restaurant that was empty but for us. A woman worked behind the counter, and we took up three of the place's four tables: Alexandra and me at one, the guy from Nikolaevsk at a second, and Martinez at a third. By the time we started talking, Alexandra's friend had started reading what appeared to be a Russian-language newspaper.

"He is one of us," she said, head bowed. "A son of Nikolaevsk." She winced when she said it, but I couldn't tell whether her concern was more for the shame of her fellow villager being wanted by the FBI or a fear of leaving the village to talk. As far as I could tell, both were playing on her mind.

"And his name is Anthony or…"

"Vitali Nikolaevsk. He is Old Believer. We all have this name." She tapped a sugar packet against the table.

The woman who worked here hadn't approached us as we'd come in. She just nodded to Alexandra and that was all. Now she brought out a pot of coffee and set down two thick white mugs. She poured them full and left us with a small metal pitcher of cream before she went to do the same for Martinez and the guard.

I stirred sugar and cream into my coffee more out of habit than desire. Getting something solid about the Daylight Killer had me more keyed up than anything had in a long time. My leg jittered under the table. My hand hurt, but I didn't care. Alexandra was already ten times better than Andrews. She wasn't rushing to tell me anything.

I sipped the coffee, noting a thin film of oil along its top. Not enough to stop me from drinking it.

"He grew up like us," she said. "Same. Work in village, tend farms, take care of animals. All same. But *him*." She turned to the man then, and he casually folded his paper in half, set it down next to his untouched coffee, and pushed his chair back. He stood and walked out of the restaurant. I heard his boots hitting the wood porch but not the stairs.

"He will wait. He does not want to hear."

"Who is he?"

"Husband," she said, her accent getting thicker the more we spoke. "He does not think I should be telling you. She would *never*." Alexandra tilted her head back toward their town. "But I must let you know if it can help. If it can help out girls."

"How do you know it's him? Who's been doing this?"

"I know *him*," she said. "When he was young, we like sister and brother. Different parents, yes, but we work together in field. Then, after he turn fifteen, he only work with animals. First sheep and then the cows." Now she looked up and our eyes met. Hers were wet; they shone. "He kill cow first. *They*—" she said this with displeasure, "they let him watch slaughter and then he want to try. But they wouldn't let. Only the old butcher, he do this.

"Then they found calf in field, slaughtered, slashed, meat eaten in the night by coyote and bear." She pursed her lips as though this caused great pain. "*Waste*. We cannot eat after scavengers, and this calf we need for village. Many men upset. She *very* upset."

"Who is she?" I had to ask it, even if I knew.

"Nina." Alexandra tilted her head back toward Nikolaevsk. "This woman you saw. She make our decisions. Waste is worst thing we can have."

I glanced over toward Martinez, but he was intent on the man outside.

"What happened to Vitali?"

More pursed lips and Alexandra shaking her head. "First, she cut him to remind." She held her hand out toward me, but instead of marking her palm lengthwise, as I'd expected, she marked it sideways, along one of the creases.

"When he do it again, she tell him to leave. He exile. We all wait. Niki"—she nodded at her husband—"drive him outside of town and leave him on highway. He not welcome back."

"When was this?"

She shook her head. "Not long. Maybe three weeks."

"You sure?"

"Oh, yes. I am sure this is fact."

"What do you mean, did it again?"

"He kill sheep. Tie it up and slit throat. Almost cut off head."

I wrote it down, wondering whether there was more, something about five years ago.

I asked, "How old is Vitali now?"

"Now he eighteen."

"Has he left your village for any length of time before this?"

"No."

Even if he had, no way a kid murdered these women at thirteen.

"Where is he now?"

"This I do not know. Why I come to you. He is not of our world now, but part of yours. For this I want to warn."

"Are there—Have there been any others?"

"What?"

"Ones you've had to exile?"

"No."

"Never?"

"No."

Now her face looked calmer, as though getting this off her chest had brought her some peace. But I felt the opposite; any excitement I'd had about getting new details was gone, leaving only curiosity about what didn't add up.

"Why did she cut his hand?"

Alexandra shrugged as though this weren't important. "This we do. It is punishment."

"Nina does this?"

She nodded.

I showed her my left hand, traced across its width. "And she always cuts like this?"

"Yes."

"Who did it before her? Who was in charge of things before Nina?"

Now she looked around her, uncertain. I heard the door chimes behind me. "This I do not know," she said.

I showed her my bandaged right hand, thinking about tearing off the gauze to show her what Andrews had done, even if that wouldn't make a point. For some reason, I wanted her to see the wound.

Then Niki was beside me saying something in Russian, and Alexandra stood up.

"I have said too much."

"Wait. I—" She waited for me while I took a deep breath. "Do you have a picture of Vitali?"

She said she didn't, that they didn't believe in this technology.

"I need you to sit with an artist to give us a sketch of Vitali. Can you do that? He will draw what you say."

She hesitated, and I added, "This is important. It could save lives."

CHAPTER 23

We were in the car again, back on the highway headed north toward Anchorage.

Alexandra had agreed to meet with our sketch artist from Homer the following day, Sunday, at three o'clock in the afternoon.

Now I just had to make sure he'd be there. I was trying to call back to the Homer PD, but my phone had no reception.

Something was off about Martinez; he sucked his teeth as he drove, his face pinched. "She's lying," he said finally.

"About what?"

"There's more to it, more she doesn't want us to know."

I put my phone back into my purse and read down my notes again. "There's no way this kid killed Samantha Parker. And the others from '06, not those either."

He nodded. "What I'm saying. That there's more."

"The hand?"

"At least. You see the way that guy was watching everything? Did you see *his* hands?"

"He wore gloves."

Now he bobbed his shoulders. He hit the steering wheel with his palm. "What I'm saying, Harding. *Exactly.*"

"No. I don't think so." I bit the inside of my cheek. The sun was beating down into the front seat now, and I lowered the visor in front of me. It didn't help.

"What?"

"You're saying the whole town is in on this?"

"No. Huh-uh. I'm just saying there's more to her story, more details about these Old Believers and their village that she isn't telling us. You know?"

I did know. Martinez was saying some of the same things I felt. I wanted to go back and ask Andrews if his man had had an accent, if he could confirm his age again. But, shit, I knew it myself that the man I'd seen running with us wasn't eighteen.

"What about Andrews? Is he telling the truth?"

Martinez nodded. The road ahead of us was two lanes and occasionally there was room to pass, but the need never arose.

"Jason Andrews is just a two-time loser," he said. "That idiot's lucky to have a truck he can drive and two dimes to rub together to buy beer."

"But his story fits together."

"Whether this girl's right at all about the kid she's talking about, he's different from the guy who paid Andrews to cut you. And there's no way he did anything in '06. So…"

I waited. "So?"

He shrugged. "None of this means shit, and we're scratching up the wrong tree trunk to get nowhere."

I let that sit for a while as we made our way up the Sterling Highway. Then I said, "Scratching up a tree trunk? You get that in Ohio?"

Martinez laughed. "One of the guys at the Salty Dog said it, told me we were scratching up the wrong tree trunk. I figured I'd give it a try."

"Who? Who said it?"

"Just some guy. It's in my notes somewhere. He was drunk."

"But wrong tree trunk? That's odd, don't you think? What tree did he say we should be scratching up?"

He shrugged again. "Actually, he didn't."

"But don't you think that's strange? Do you remember what he looked like?" I dug into the back pocket of Martinez's seat, pulling out his notepad, and then started going through it.

He was eyeing the pages as he drove, and when I got to the right one, he stopped me. "There," he said, pointing to the center of the page. "That part."

I read the notes he had: *Alaskan. Hat/sweater. Tattoos.*

"Who was this guy? *Tattoos?*"

He bit his lip. "Shit if I know. Just that I thought he had some fucked-up tats."

"Did it occur to you that this might have been the guy Andrews was describing? Did you see him by the trucks?"

"Who by the trucks?"

I tapped the pad. "This guy."

"No. Huh-uh. Didn't see him."

I turned back to the pad. *Wrong tree*, it said. I circled that.

"Doesn't it seem weird to you that he said this?"

"Not any more than the rest of the things in that bar."

I couldn't argue with that. The rest of the page was empty. I showed it to Martinez.

He said, "That was when you got cut."

CHAPTER 24

By the time we saw the first buildings over two stories tall, signaling the start of urban Anchorage, it was after seven o'clock and both Martinez and I were beat. I *felt* tired, and I was pissed from all the time in the car, but in truth when I got out to walk around, the bright sun made me feel energized again. Not a single streetlight was on; it might as well have been lunchtime or one o'clock in the afternoon.

Martinez dropped me off at my hotel, and I went up to change out of the clothes I'd bought at Homer's hardware emporium. In truth, they'd served their purpose and then some. I hesitated half a beat before tossing them into the trash. No way I could ever wear these in San Francisco or on the job here in Anchorage. But maybe they'd have another use. I decided to put them aside in a drawer for the time being.

I put the suit I'd worn down to Homer into the hotel's dry-cleaning bag and called down for them to pick it up. In my suitcase, I'd brought just one other suit, the one with the skirt, and so I had to go with that, Linstrom and Owens or not.

Since I'd promised Linstrom that I'd get to the office, I put it on and went down to have a cab take me over.

At the Bureau, Linstrom had gone for the night but left a note that I should call him. I ripped it off the gray canvas wall of the empty cubicle I'd been temporarily assigned.

Another message was clipped next to it, letting me know the sketch artist from Homer would be at the restaurant the next day to meet Alexandra. So that was good.

His sketch from the Andrews session sat next to my phone on the desk. The drawing was rough because it had been faxed over; whatever clarity it had in the original was lost. On the other hand, at least now the fax machine here printed to flat paper. My last time in Alaska, in 2006, they had one that still printed onto a spool of the thin, shiny stuff. Awesome, really, as relics went, but not too handy—you never got those sheets to stop rolling up on you when you tried to read them.

The picture looked grainy and a little generic, like the face could be many people instead of only a few. What I saw was a man with a baseball hat, and the sketch artist had done his best to put features into the face. The two eyes pressed together and the eyebrows were thick. The man in this drawing had a beard, and as I looked at him, I tried to imagine if he had helped me down from the old trucker's door. That guy had had his hand on my elbow, and I'd been too wrapped up in the moment to notice if I felt anything odd. Perhaps he gave me an extra squeeze, perhaps not. I'd stood right next to him and missed him completely. He'd been *right there*.

The Daylight Killer knew my name, had painted it on walls, killed a woman in an apartment that mirrored my own, and managed to have someone cut my hand. He had talked to Martinez and touched my elbow. He was getting so close to me, but I was no closer to him than the bland drawing in my hand, some spotty details about strange tattoos, and a weird story about a too-young suspect from a strange Russian village.

There was one more thing: I knew we both had vertical cuts along the palm of our right hand. I had twelve stitches and a hand covered in gauze and bandages to remind me. A shiver ran up my spine, and I sat down hard in my chair. He had done this to me.

At the sound of a cough behind me, I spun around—embarrassed, and maybe too fast. Both of the agents standing before me jumped back as if I'd lunged at them.

"Jesus, Harding," one said, "you high-strung, or what?"

The other said, "Take another Vicodin for that hand."

I did my best to smile. In front of me were two agents out of the DC office who looked exactly how you'd expect agents to look. Anyone on the street would mistake them for the men in black from *The Matrix*. I almost expected one to say, "*Mr. Anderson*," in that familiar deadpan.

I forced a smile and stood up. "Hello, gentlemen. Jessica Harding. It's nice to meet you."

Each put out his hand in turn and shook mine.

"Withers," the first said.

"Bos," said the second.

I nodded.

"Dinner?" Withers asked.

"I could eat."

"Exceptional," said Bos.

They both turned and started up the hall, away from my cube. I took the message from Linstrom and my notes from Homer and put them into my briefcase along with the sketch artist's drawing. As I did, I took one last look at his face. It didn't give me quite the chill I'd felt before, and it *definitely* wasn't an eighteen-year-old, but the drawing made me feel *something*. That chill was still with me. It was inside my flesh.

"I hope you like fish," one of the agents said—Withers or Bos, I couldn't tell—as he held the door for me.

They chose a fancy seafood restaurant in the northwest part of town, usually the one we recommended for folks from far away who didn't care about money. Since it would be their office picking up the tab and not San Francisco or Anchorage, I didn't care.

From our table, they both had a great view of the Knik Arm and across the water to Point MacKenzie. Bos ordered the halibut and Withers the salmon. I ordered a burger. Old habits die hard.

They'd each put away a salad and a Diet Coke before they started asking questions.

"So, your hand," Withers said. "Let's start with you telling us about that."

"What's to tell? I got cut. It's not too bad."

"But it *is* bad. You spent a night in the hospital." They glanced at each other.

I shrugged. For the second time that day, I wanted to rip off the bandages and show someone what was underneath. A waiter walked by, and I stopped him to order a Bloody Mary. Both Withers and Bos had their eyebrows way up when I turned back.

I smiled again. "Just to ease my nerves," I said. "It's been a long day. And no, I'm not mixing it with Vicodin."

Bos nodded. "Well, all right. Fair enough. Actually, I'll have a beer myself. That sounds good."

Withers seconded the motion, and the waiter went away. "What we really want to know about is the situation with Senator Parker's daughter. Let's start with everything you have there."

"Good idea," I said. "First, I'm sure you realize that the evidence connects her murder to the larger profile of an ongoing case."

They nodded eagerly, wanting more.

Withers said, "You're talking about this serial killer investigation. Evidence connects this back to several murders in 2006 that you were the lead investigator on. All women killed during white nights."

Bos said, "And what can I tell Senator Parker of your estimation for *when* we will have this matter solved?"

I tried to look both of them in the eyes at the same time and couldn't, not as directly as I wanted to when I answered. Instead, I looked right at Withers first. "Yes," I said. I turned to Bos. "That's not as easy to answer."

The waiter came back and set down my Bloody Mary, topped with a nice piece of celery and a big green olive. I thanked him and sucked down about a third of it through the straw. Withers and Bos didn't touch their beers.

"You worked on this for six months in 2006 and were then relocated to the San Francisco office, where you've acquitted yourself well since that time."

"*Quite* well," Withers added.

I could see waiters coming over with our food and hoped the agents would dive in as they had with the salads.

"Thanks. I've had some luck. You two must know how an agent's investigative skills improve as you're with the Bureau."

Two waiters came around, plating our table, and both agents inhaled deeply from the steam over their meals. I'd forgotten how good the fish was here in Alaska—not something anyone should ever forget. The case was distracting me; I was off. I smelled my burger and felt dumb for not ordering fish, but the time in the hospital had me craving a dose of red meat.

"Actually—" Withers forked a potato into his mouth and carved a large bite out of his salmon. "We mostly do triage, you could say. Managing expectations and tamping down situations. We're not investigators, *per se*."

Bos nodded, more preoccupied with the food than the case. "It's really the nature of the particular beast in Washington."

I cut my burger in half and poured a dipping pond of ketchup onto my plate. I'd gone with a side salad instead of fries, my one waistline-saving grace.

Bos was shaking his head. "You can imagine the caliber of assholes we have to deal with in the capital." He ate a forkful of halibut and, through his chewing, said, "But it has its perks." He raised his eyebrows, closing his eyes and humming at the taste of the food.

Withers said, "This really is fabulous salmon. You should try this." He angled his plate in my direction, but I shook my head.

Despite my own expectations, I was beginning to like these two. Boring or by the book, they wanted to taste good food and that made them endearing—a lot more than if they were just out to spend Bureau dollars to show off. It was a Saturday night in Anchorage, damn it, and they wanted to have a good time.

"Let me try it this way," I said. "You can tell Senator Parker that we're now closer to a solid suspect in the Daylight Killer case than we've ever been before. We don't understand this five-year hiatus, but several key factors are matches: the white nights, as you said, the barbed wire, and a few others. In the last few days, I've interviewed at least three witnesses who've seen the man we believe to be responsible. My partner may have encountered him personally during a canvas of witnesses at a bar."

Both of them perked up, as if this information was almost as good as the food.

Withers waved for another round of drinks. They still wore their ties tight, but I could sense a loosening in their attitudes. Even with these two, Alaska could have that effect: being so far away from everything you knew and were used to, where all the rules seemed to have changed, you couldn't help but think differently. That, or the fact that it was after nine o'clock and the sky outside resembled a sunny afternoon, made you want to cut yourself some slack.

CHAPTER 25

I didn't tell the agents that I'd seen the suspect myself or thought I had. *That* was a story I didn't want to explain. So I avoided the chase and focused instead on Andrews's interview and what he'd given up.

I was also sensitive about mentioning anything involving Alexandra or Nikolaevsk. The idea of a gun-toting old sect of Russian Orthodoxy being involved was just too messy to bring up in a pre-packaged way these guys could port back to DC. Never mind the political implications.

"What I'd like to talk with you two about is resources. It hurt my investigation that I didn't have a chance to fly down to Homer on the plane."

They waived this away as though the waiter had just asked if there was any problem with the food. "Simple misunderstanding," Bos said. "Any expenses that you deem necessary—if the Anchorage office cannot approve, or if San Francisco isn't involved—you send them directly to us."

Withers smiled. "Let's just say Senator Parker isn't on the budget committee, but in these matters, he might as well be. Tell your friend Martinez that he won't be needing to drive you anywhere unless you deem it necessary."

I considered this uneasily. It was the response I had wanted, but I wasn't thrilled. The main hurdle was equality, having the resources at my disposal. On the other hand, if our stop in Nikolaevsk was any indication, being on the ground had its advantages. So if I smelled a lead that we needed a car for, I'd get it. If I wanted to move around quickly, which was a big advantage in a state where everything was larger than in any other, then access to a plane promised big benefits.

Even if I cringed at the idea of leaving solid ground.

Bos pushed away his plate, having cleaned it of all but a few dollops of sauce. "Speaking of Martinez, how's he proving himself thus far?" he asked. "Will he continue to be useful?"

I nodded. "Agent Martinez is a bit green, but I like his instincts. I'd like to keep him involved."

"Fair enough."

Bos said, "You realize, of course, that Anchorage is also running a smaller-scale investigation at this point. But because of how you've proven yourself, we may bring that to an end."

"In favor of yours," Withers said.

"Of course," Bos added, "and if you need assistance with lab work or forensics, absolutely make your best use of what the office can offer you here. Or if you need more…" He trailed off but the intention was clear.

I told them I would be in touch, adding that a blood expert by the name of Owens would be helpful, though I hadn't had a chance to consult him yet.

Bos said, "Anyone who knows the work you did in '06, go ahead and use what they can offer."

When our waiter came back and asked for dessert orders, they studied the small menus and chose molten chocolate cake and chocolate fudge mud pie. They looked at me as if genuinely expecting me to go whole hog the way they were. I shook my head and ordered a decaf.

Bos said, "Never know how I'll manage to sleep tonight if it's still light out. I feel like this should be lunch."

"Or brunch." Withers laughed.

I resisted making the point that they'd each put away a good two meals' worth of food already.

"You'll manage," I said. "It's actually not that bad when you close the blinds."

They nodded as if that made them happier than they already were. Then they informed me that they were leaving in the morning, and I should do everything in my power to keep them updated. I told them I planned to.

CHAPTER 26

At the hotel, I looked at the clock and decided not to bother calling Linstrom; he'd be up, no doubt. Though the light coming in the window gave me the energy to keep the night going, my hand felt like it'd been cut wide open—because it *had*. I took a pill instead, and went to sleep.

During the night I dreamed I lived in a bell tower surrounded by chimes. They rang at all hours of day and night, though visually I couldn't tell the difference. The tower was at the top of a very tall hill or a mountain somewhere—high enough that I felt edgy about its height. It was not San Francisco, though the tower might have been Coit Tower transplanted to Alaska. I never had the chance to rest in this dream world because of all the chimes and bells. When I woke up, I felt groggy and exhausted. Someone was banging on my door and the phone beside my bed and my cell were both ringing.

Martinez yelled through the door, "Let me in, Harding. We got a break!"

I struggled into a hotel robe and made my way to the door, happy at least that he had stopped banging. It was a Sunday morning and despite the bright sun outside I knew one thing: it was way too early to be up.

I opened the door, and he pushed past me to come inside. He threw my suitcase onto the bed and started shoving things into it.

"What's happening?"

"We're leaving," he said. "Couple of hikers found a dead body down in Kachemak Bay State Park, right across the water from

Homer. Middle of the woods and this body's all cut up on a trail. It's a fucking mess. Blood everywhere."

Our plan was to fly down from Anchorage in a simple four-seater floatplane. We had to take a plane if we wanted to get there before night. Otherwise we'd be waiting in Homer for high tide and a boat to take us across the water. By plane, we would cover the Kenai Peninsula, pass Homer, and cross Kachemak Bay in less than an hour, then put in at one of the coves between the mountains of the Chugach range.

Two hikers had found a carved up body late Saturday night on a trail about a mile into Kachemak Bay State Park—a boy. Not going after a woman was a first for our killer, definitely strange, but the rest of the scene—the blood work, the mess, the barbed wire— were all so consistent with the other scenes that even Martinez had recognized it as *him*.

Why a boy? Why now? I didn't know. But the whole thing got a lot more interesting when Martinez gave me one critical detail: one of the boy's hands had a scar across the palm.

Martinez drove us from my hotel to the water and we went out onto a dock to board the plane. As long as we were on the water, I felt fine. But I knew we'd be leaving the ground soon, and that had my stomach doing twists. In a big airplane I can avoid the windows and convince myself I'm just in a big box. I still get nauseated when we go up, make dips, or have turbulence, but I can spare myself from looking at the ground as we leave it.

Here, on what basically amounted to a metal tube with a propeller and skis, I'd have no choice but to see out. Even if I closed my eyes completely, I couldn't help but know we were high up in the air. And there was no way I could keep my eyes shut for the whole ride.

I got into my seat, pulled my seatbelt tight, and did my best to breathe. When Martinez was in, too, he closed the door. I gave some hard consideration to getting out right then and driving. But I knew I couldn't show fear. That's the first trap in a man's world: let them know you're a woman with a fear, something irrational like heights or a plane, and they come after you. They'd piled on me up in '06 like a school of sharks to blood—all that over my nerves— but I'd learned my lesson there. No closing my eyes or showing my fear of heights.

I counted breaths. The pilot told us to put on ear protection, and then he started the propeller. I was all sweaty palms and clawed armrests.

As a kid, I'd been afraid of heights. If I got near the edge of anything high up, I'd feel as if I was about to go right over it. Even inside a building with a very high ceiling, like a church, my knees buckled. I couldn't stand. Something closed inside me whenever I had to look up or down and see a great distance.

I knew I had a problem when we did Project Adventure in sixth grade. You had to climb up a wall, stand on a little outcrop about ten feet up—all this while being belayed by the teacher—and then jump to catch onto a trapeze with your hands. I made the jump again and again but never caught the trapeze. I couldn't keep my eyes open to see it. I knew the feel of it hitting my hands, but couldn't see when to grab hold.

I tried to cure myself, working to get rid of this weakness. In my teens I climbed the fire escape at one of the places my mother stayed, catching the lowest rung by scrambling up from a chair and then willing myself to the first window—the second floor. Then I kept climbing. When I'd cleared the railing of the second floor's fire escape, I had four or five feet of open ladder between the second and third floors. This I feared most. No one to belay me here, no ropes; just the hard ground of the backyard some twenty or more feet down. I clung to the thin, black metal rungs, felt their rust, and refused to look down. Just me up there. I kept the churning inside me, tried to keep it in check.

In my twenties, I started rock climbing, even went ice climbing on a glacier once or twice up in Alaska, just a few hours east of Anchorage. At first I'd felt pure adrenaline fear, like a shot of cocaine, as I got higher. Looking down left me weak in all my limbs. My hands sweat. But it got better: I became used to the workouts, the muscle movements, and climbing from my legs, not my arms. I became good at the sport but still hated to look down from any height. I got through by focusing only on the wall in front of me.

All of this to say that I'd had my fears of heights through the years. It still wasn't something I had gotten over. As the plane took off, I watched Martinez stare out the window. As long as he wasn't watching me, I didn't have to fake it as much. I gripped the armrests with my short fingernails, breathed through my mouth.

The pilot looked back at me. "It'll be okay," he said through the mic.

"I'm fine."

Martinez looked over.

"Really. Just fine here."

The trip took less than an hour, and I knew every minute. I hadn't eaten, which meant I'd have nothing to throw up if I lost it, nothing but bile. A small consolation. When we were passing over the Spit, Martinez tapped his window, and I steeled myself for a look down. With my teeth clenched and my stomach in a knot, I saw the Fishing Hole and the Salty Dog. I saw where the trucks parked and where we'd chased Andrews. Then the plane banked, and I shut my eyes tight, tasting metal.

CHAPTER 27

We finally put down into Halibut Cove Lagoon around ten a.m. and I let go of my armrests. The pilot ferried us up to the dock, where a park ranger waited. He had on the hat and official uniform and looked every bit the part, with a bushy beard and some serious hiking boots at the bottom of his brown pants. He had no idea how glad I was to see him.

When I stepped out onto the dock, my legs felt like rubber. I'd worn my running shoes for the excursion, the closest thing I had to what I'd need on these trails, and it was good because I'd have never stayed up in heels. I held my knees and breathed in the clean mountain air. The dock shimmied from the ripple of the plane's wake. I held the ranger's arm. So much for not showing weakness.

Martinez wore good hiking boots, just like an agent who'd spent enough time in the Great Land to catch on. On the other hand, I had on my skirt suit because the pantsuit was at the cleaners after what it'd gone through in Homer. This, and my sneakers. Not only fashionable but functional as well. Just great.

I held Martinez's arm as we followed the ranger up the ramp and onto solid ground. The plane and pilot would stay here for us, waiting for our next destination, my next chance to gag. Once on solid ground, I let go of Martinez and stood up straight.

"Get me?" I asked him. He looked confused, so I waved my finger in his face. "You don't mention this. *Ever.*"

I raised my eyebrows, waiting for him to agree.

"Got it," he said. "Boss. You got a thing. Won't mention it."

"Being human is what it is, René. We're all just trying here. Get me?" His first name took the smile right off his face and made him get serious fast.

Now I smiled. "Problem?"

He didn't answer, just walked up the trail after the ranger.

At a far dock, I saw a police boat from the Homer PD, but no officers in sight.

Kachemak Bay State Park could only be accessed by water. Only a handful of companies in Homer ran water taxis out here. These went twice daily at high tide—you needed the full swell to get to the dock.

"We see a lot of hikers out here with handguns and rifles," the ranger told us. He took us into his main station house, a room no bigger than ten feet by ten feet, adorned with enough taxidermied animals to make the great white hunter proud. "So once in a great while we wind up with somebody shot by accident, but *definitely* nothing like this."

On a table in the center of the room, he spread out a detailed trail map. He put his finger on our current location and then showed us where the hikers found the body, along with the trail route we would take to get out there. "Homer police been out looking at this scene for a couple hours, but ain't none of them come back yet. Not sure what's taking them so long."

I could imagine. Even if they had dealt with the carnage at the Fishing Hole the other night, that was relatively mild compared with a full crime scene left behind by our Daylight Killer. When I'd seen my first as a young agent…well, I actually still experienced moments when it popped back into my mind's eye.

For this scene, we had yet to see any pictures, but the reports the hikers gave involved a lot of blood and a general mess, something undoubtedly man-made. "Knife work" was the note that stuck with me.

"So you two ready to hike out there?" The ranger was looking at me.

"You bet." I'd been staring at the map, at our position at Halibut Cove Lagoon. The name of the cove being attributed to a fish didn't surprise me. What did surprise me was the name of the next cove west: China Poot Bay. What the hell was that about?

As we set out, the ranger offered me a walking stick, which I declined. Martinez thought about making a crack at this, I could see, but the look on my face stopped him cold.

"Good decision," I said.

We had a good climb ahead of us, rises and drops in elevation that involved switchbacks on both sides. The ranger told us we'd be hiking for at least an hour. He would lead us out personally.

I stopped to peel off my tights as soon as I warmed up. Alaska wasn't hot this time of year by any stretch, but once I got into the workout, I wanted to be comfortable. For all the time on planes, in cars, and at the hospital, some exercise felt better than anything I could ask for.

As I was trailing the ranger up an incline of steady switchbacks, I noticed the gun on his belt but not a can of pepper spray for the bears.

"Don't much think I need it," he said. "They see you, they'd just as likely make tracks as stick around. And believe me, they see us way before we see them."

I believed him. What had struck me strangest when I lived up here was the way everyone tried to kill his or her yearly bear *and* a moose. Each citizen was entitled to one of each, per year, which basically came down to the summer season and part of fall, and they went after them with vigor. Most filled their freezer with the butchered meat and ate that for the rest of the year.

The people I'd met even had opinions about what time of year to kill a bear for the sweetest meat, but they'd go after a moose in the forest any chance they got. They would always carry out what they killed, too. In this sense, the typical Alaskan wasn't so different from the citizens of Nikolaevsk in their abhorrence of waste. With a winter so long, and so much cold to look forward to, you thought about supplying yourself for it every bit of the year it wasn't on your back.

We passed the Homer police hiking out about halfway to our destination. There were two of them, both men, and they looked pretty green around the gills, their faces well beyond white.

"Bad scene out there?" the ranger asked.

One said, "Ayyuh," and that was all.

I didn't bother to ask for a full description, knowing we'd be there ourselves soon enough. I did look at a handful of the pictures they had taken on a digital camera, and that was enough to know it was our killer. There was blood everywhere. But what I was most looking for, I couldn't find.

"Where's a shot of the face?" I asked.

Both cops shook their heads. "Huh-uh," one said.

I didn't see anything in the photos that wasn't blood, flesh, or bloody leaves.

Then I saw the eyes. It was a head, but the skin had been flayed, peeled back just like someone might do to a bear to skin it for a rug.

"Jesus," I said.

"Sure enough," one cop said. "That's what I been thinking."

I thought I could still smell the scent of vomit coming off his boots.

CHAPTER 28

Then both Homer officers were gone, hiking off in their blue uniforms and orange jackets, rushing to get back to their boat and bring in the evidence. They'd left another officer out there to guard the body from bears, and the whole carcass would be on a coroner's table by tomorrow. But first we'd have our look at the scene.

"Hope you brought the good camera," I told Martinez.

He nodded. "They didn't look too good."

"No lie there. You sure you're ready for this?"

Martinez didn't answer. The ranger said, "Tell you the truth, I might just wait a few dozen yards out of sight. I seen this once already, and that's enough."

"Your prerogative."

"Shit, I see dead moose and bear carcass all the time. But this?" He shook his head. "Just not my cup of joe."

We hiked until we got to the yellow police tape. It closed off the trail, but no one had made an attempt to point hikers around it or otherwise make a detour. There wasn't going to be anyone else out this way for a while.

The third cop came out to the tape line and held it up for us to enter. I went first, and Martinez followed.

"Blood trail starts here." The officer, whose badge read PHILLIPS, showed us where blood had spattered the leaves of the low shrubs. "Nothing out of the ordinary at first. Just like he hiked in, calm as you please." The ranger had said the same thing about the absence of marks on the trail as we were coming in. "Then here's where the trouble started."

"Strange." I stopped and went back, asked the ranger whether anyone had reserved a cabin for the previous night, and he said he would check back at the station but didn't remember off the top of his head.

When I turned around, I knew Martinez had ventured in far enough to see the scene. His face had gone an extra shade of white and his mouth looked wet. He was grimacing, as if he wanted to squeeze his eyes shut and not see anything for a while.

"It'll be all right," I said. "Why don't you give me the camera and wait with the ranger?"

He took the camera out of his backpack and handed it to me but wouldn't leave. "Huh-uh. I need to see this. Part of the job."

"Fair enough." I walked past him. The trail had gone muddy in this section, and I had to stay outside the edge of the mud, trying to keep my sneakers dry. I walked up onto the grass, what there was of it. Mostly rocks and shrubs made up the terrain. Trees circled us; the forest was thick. Around a turn, I saw blood, and then the body. Like in the photos, blood had sprayed the plants, dried, and congealed on the leaves. It covered the rocks that I saw, spattered across them, and made a mess on the base of a tree. The boy was propped up against its trunk, both arms down by his sides, and his shirt was stripped off to his waist. From the top of his head, his skin was flayed back off his skull and left there like a mask someone had cut open and not fully removed. I could see brown hair, the top of a head turned inside out, and holes in the face for his eyes.

"I'm going to be sick," Martinez said.

"Keep saying that to yourself. It'll keep you from puking, I think."

Martinez said it again. Then he stepped back and wobbled. Soon I could hear him throwing up.

The boy's right hand had been cut off and propped up on a stick, with its palm facing out to us, almost as though he was waving. But he couldn't be waving, because he was dead. Instead it was like *he* was waving at us, waving at *me* to show me what he'd left behind. The hand had a horizontal cut across it, just like Alexandra had shown me in the restaurant the day before. By the look of the cut, it wasn't more than a month or two old.

"Vitali Nikolaevsk," I said. I didn't like that this made sense to me.

CHAPTER 29

I stepped around the scene and got close to the hand, bent down, and snapped a good picture. This was going to be something I would remember, but I wanted proof of it to add to the file.

"You ever see any cut like that one on a hand before this?" I asked Officer Phillips.

"Before you?"

"Before me."

"Well, yours was up and down, not side to side like his."

I waited him out.

"Read it in the report," he said.

"How long you been on this job?"

"Four years."

"Okay," I said. "Thank you."

But then he said something that stopped me. "I heard about one other time, though. Case where a kid had a cut on his hand. But that was a long ways back."

I had my pad out from writing notes about the scene, and I made a note to ask other Homer police about what he'd just said. "Any idea when?"

"Years ago. Before I came on."

I asked him who I should talk to about it, what officer might still be around who'd remember the case.

"Officer Cope," he said. "That guy remembers everything."

I made a note of the name, underlined it three times on its own separate page in my notebook, and wrote *hand* next to it and circled that.

What else did I need to see about the body? Why else had I come all this way to add to my book of horrors?

I snapped my own set of pictures of the scene, hoping I wouldn't come across any writing. The barbed wire was present here, twisted around the still-intact wrist and binding it to a root. More of it had been wrapped around the boy's calf, tying his leg down to the tree's roots.

Below the waist, none of the boy's clothes had been removed. He wore canvas pants, heavy ones like I'd noticed on the men in Nikolaevsk, and I knew they wouldn't have a brand in their waistline if I checked. They'd been homemade in his small town. Same for the shirt, which hung around his middle: it was a faded plaid, cut from some thick flannel that came cheap by the roll. His boots weren't fancy, but had been purchased in a store, though perhaps for another boy, who'd grown out of them before their usefulness was up.

All of it announced itself as the attire of a simple life lived on the land. It made sense to me—too much, perhaps. I wondered how far down this rabbit hole I would have to go before I caught this killer, and what it'd take to come back up from it all when I did. In five years, I'd just come back to the surface of the last hole he had led me down, and that wasn't as messy as this one was starting to be. He had changed in the interim, gotten angrier, more ruthless with his kills, more barbaric. Where had he been in that time, I wondered. And what was he doing? Or what was it doing to him?

I kept looking around, taking pictures, and started finding words—his hallmark. He'd written in blood on rocks, on leaves, even on a piece of bark or two. He had left behind messages, knowing they wouldn't make sense but also knowing I would find them.

I knew why I was still looking, even after Phillips went back up the trail to sit down, even after I could smell the smoke of his cigarette wafting through the leaves. I would find it, even though I knew I didn't want to.

Then there it was: my own name.

Jess.

He had written it on a rock, in small letters, in just such a way that you would have to look really close at the scene to find it. And I had, as he knew I would. I felt a shiver go through me. And I realized the two of us were closer in all this than I thought—closer than I wanted to be.

When I saw my name, something changed; now I saw all of the writing more clearly, as if seeing this smaller set of important letters made me see many more small letters I hadn't noticed. And then, next to the boy's body, I noticed a word I hadn't seen before: *fake.*

I stared at that for a few moments, looking at what was left of Anthony or Vitali or whatever he was called. With his head stripped back like a trophy, his hand waving at me, and his body so clearly destroyed, I knew the kid had struck a nerve. The Daylight Killer wasn't pleased with what this boy had done. Maybe that included killing Adina Howard. Maybe our man came down to see the body just like I had, found this kid posing and taking credit for some of *his* work and didn't like it. Or maybe this kid reminded my guy too much of himself.

Adina Howard hadn't been tied with barbed wire. Just the hook and the different way the muscle fibers had been ripped. Her death was reminiscent of Tina Bruce's five years ago, but not an exact replica, as the coroner had said. Maybe I should have caught on to that faster. Or maybe they had worked together, and my killer had had enough of this young partner. Either way, it didn't matter now.

I had found what I came for, seen what he wanted me to see. Now it was time to find Officer Cope and ask some questions about the past.

CHAPTER 30

Martinez didn't seem so bad off by the time I found him on the trail.

"You okay?" I asked.

"You know I'll be fine."

As we went on ahead, I asked the ranger to give us a few minutes. He said sure and walked on. I hoped he'd be at his cabin when I saw him next, preparing a sheet of names to tell me who'd been out this way in the last couple of days and who had reserved the public-use cabins. I also wanted to check with the water taxis to see who they took out on Friday and Saturday.

"What do you think?" I asked Martinez.

"It's the kid from Nikolaevsk, right?"

"That hand sure looks like it." I filled him in on the writing, up to the word *fake* but not including my name. "Maybe if this boy killed Adina Howard, it raised some anger with someone else."

Martinez looked as though he didn't want to hear what I had to say, but he was resigned to it, too.

"So our man is still out here, and now he's not just killing women."

"Yeah," I said. "It looks that way."

The ranger had my names ready when we got back to the station, which also turned out to be his house and a museum of sorts for tourists to see the animals they'd encounter in the park. Situated among the displays was the sign-in book for the cabins, and behind a door, the residence he shared with his wife and two girls.

"You all be careful out here."

The ranger smiled. "Believe me. We've got plenty of firepower, and my girls all know how to use it. We'll be all right."

I wanted to tell him how dangerous this killer was, and that he'd been right outside this cabin, right outside on the trail—the only trail that led into the woods.

I said, "He's been here at some point. This man. And he's dangerous. He's killed eight or nine girls and women already, and now this young man. Who knows what the hell he'll turn to next."

The ranger nodded. "I seen what he did. And I know how to protect mine. Maybe I'll keep the cabins closed for another few days to keep out the campers."

"I'd recommend it. At least."

The names on his list didn't look familiar, of course, except for one: Holcomb Parker, which was Samantha's father's name, and the senator certainly wasn't planning a visit out to this part of the woods.

I tapped the list with a finger. "Whose handwriting is this?"

"That? That's my daughter's. This one must have booked online."

"Where is this cabin?"

"It's a nice one. Big Elk Cabin is out by the lake, farther down that trail we were on today."

I checked Martinez to see if he was taking this all in, and he was.

"Reserved for last night."

"And do you know if anyone was out there?"

The ranger shook his head. "I was out this morning to make sure of it. Wanted to be sure no one else stumbled across the body. I went to all the cabins and that one hadn't been used. Last entry in the guest book was from the night before." He shrugged. "Just a family entry like any other. Written by one of their kids."

"I'll want to see that guest book," I said. "Any chance you can get it and fax me the last few days' sheets?"

He nodded like it wouldn't be a problem. "Sure bet. I've got a copy machine and fax in the house here. Just tell me where you want it sent." Technology was finally on my side. I couldn't help but smile as I gave him Linstrom's number in Anchorage.

As we walked back to the floatplane, I could feel the hairs rising on the back of my neck. I swore not to let it get me this time; we were just jumping across the bay to Homer to check with the water taxi outfits and find Officer Cope—less than a ten-minute ride.

We boarded the plane and it flew us low out of the lagoon and over the cove. Seeing things from just a few dozen feet up, I felt more comfortable.

"Think we could keep it like this for a while?"

The pilot nodded. "Long as we're not going far."

The water looked beautiful below us. On the shores a sprinkling of houses were all grand vacation homes for the rich and year-round getaways for people who could do their grocery shopping by boat or plane.

Everything around us seemed spectacular and gigantic, on a scale like no other. After five years in California I'd forgotten how big and amazing Alaska could be. We passed an ocean liner full of containers and a dark-colored military boat that looked like a destroyer, something from the game Battleship.

"Japanese Navy come to town, looks like," our pilot said into the microphone. "Not sure what they're up to, but that's them all right." He pointed to the destroyer. "Hate it when those Japs come around."

CHAPTER 31

I realized we'd be without a car when we set down at the Spit, and since it was a floatplane, we didn't have any other option about where to land. I wanted to head into town and find Officer Cope. We were going to need a car. The pilot radioed down to the dock for them to call us a cab.

Martinez wanted to laugh. I could see it on his face plain as day. The idea of our riding to the police station and around Homer on official FBI business in the back of a local taxi had me smiling, too. Next thing I knew, we were both laughing. Even in the cramped second row of the small airplane, with thick, cupped earphones on our heads to help quiet the sound of the engine, we were laughing there, side by side, at the ridiculousness of it all.

We didn't make eye contact, Martinez and I, and when we stopped laughing, it was all business again.

The taxi waiting for us at the dock was an old gray American sedan with loose fabric hanging down from its ceiling and windows that rolled up and down by crank—ridiculous even by Anchorage standards. The old cabby wore a baseball hat with a hook stuck into the side of its bill. It announced, "I'd rather be fishing." Of course he would.

I told him to take us to the combination police station and morgue, and we were off, driving up the Spit at nearly twenty miles an hour.

"Any luck at the Fishing Hole?" I asked.

He met my eyes in the rearview. "It's closed since that girl's body turned up. Though I suspect all the dredging they done gonna kill off the fishing for a time here anyway."

"It's too bad."

He eyed me further. "You the one got your hand cut out here other night? The federal agent, ain't you?"

I held up my gauze-wrapped hand to show him. "Any chance you were at the Salty Dog then?"

He laughed. "Nothing but the hard-up and tourists drink there. I drink at the Down East. That's a real Homer bar." He pointed off in a different direction as we reached the end of the Spit, the only one of all the four roads in Homer we hadn't been down. It would've been a charming little place, Homer, if there hadn't been a killer on the loose.

The taxi took us to the station, where I asked for Officer Cope, only to find that he'd retired some years ago. "Now you can find him at Two Sisters," the officer at the front desk told me. "That's where he spends his afternoons."

"What's that?"

"Coffee shop. Other side of town. Real nice muffins they got."

I had him call our taxi again, wishing I'd just asked him to wait, and then we were in the back of the gray sedan again, Martinez and I, avoiding the overhanging fabric with our heads and making eye contact with the driver in his rearview.

"Why didn't you say you was looking for Jeff Cope?" the driver asked. "Could of saved you the trouble."

"You know him?"

He started to answer, but I cut him off. "Sure you know him," I said.

"I'm Billy Moose. I know everybody in Homer and everything there is to know about them."

"That so?" But I didn't press him for details. For now, I was content to get to the Two Sisters and find my cop.

This time I asked Billy Moose to wait for us.

"Can't do," he said. "Got a big load of tourists to pick up over at the cruise ship."

I started to answer, ready to offer him more money, but he just laughed.

"You all too serious," he said. "Come on. I'm just *moosing* around with you." He turned around and looked at me, one toothy, too-big smile on his face, waiting for me to laugh.

Martinez and I exchanged a glance, and then we both got out of the cab.

"I'll start working on calling those water taxis," he said.

The clerk at the station had called ahead to Cope, so he was waiting for me when we showed. To my delight, he had already poured me a large coffee, and all I had to do was add cream and sugar.

Martinez went straight to the counter to evaluate the food offerings and start with his calls. Cope showed me to a table in the back.

"Officer Phillips told me you're the man who knows everything," I said as we were sitting down.

Cope tilted his head. "Not sure about that, but I'll help you best I can."

"I want to get as much as you know about Nikolaevsk, even if it isn't so much."

"That's right. Them Old Believers keep pretty much to themselves. We barely had cause to deal with them over twenty years. Fifteen and some miles up the road, at least, and most of them don't drive."

I wanted to rip the gauze off my hand for the fourth time in half as many days. "My hand got cut like this." I traced the line of the cut down my palm. "And we just found a dead boy from Nikolaevsk whose palm was cut, too. But like this, horizontally." I showed him. "I believe these cuts are some sort of punishment or ritual that happens in Nikolaevsk when one of them does wrong. You know anything about that?"

Cope looked up at me then and met my eyes. It stopped me cold.

"We had a hand like that come up," he said. "Oh, 'bout, well, I guess it's ten years gone by now." He swore. "Sorry, didn't mean to do the Bruce Springsteen on you."

"What?"

"'Glory Days.' Anyhow, these were definitely not them. We had a man here in town back then. Oh, not much older than a boy, really. He was what you call a bad seed. Kicked right out of Nikolaevsk, he was. Old Believers just didn't want him around no more. Come here looking to get work and couldn't go more than a day without starting a fight." He shook his head, stared down at the black surface of his coffee. "Just bad shit, what happened."

I asked what he meant.

"Fights. Up the Salty Dog, on boats he got hired to, this and that, Fishing Hole, anyplace really. Seems like every other day or twice a week, I'd have him back in my car, bringing him up the station to spend a night. Funny thing too was he never drank that hard, never past the legal limit. Just angry, he seemed. About angry as all get out. Pissed off at the world."

"And his hand?"

"Yeah." He glanced over toward the counter. "You sure you're not hungry? They got—Well, just about everything they make here is good, you know."

Martinez stood waiting for his order and talking into his phone. He had a pen out and his notepad.

"I'm not hungry. Tell me more about this guy. What was his name, for one?"

Cope bit his lip. "They just call him Nikolaevsk. Vitali, I guess was his first name, though I met more of those than I can shake a stick at. Seem like everyone they got over there uses that last name and most of them have the same first. Like they only got about five names among them."

I tapped my coffee mug. Suddenly I wanted more than caffeine. "We had a boy killed out in Kachemak State Park this morning, only about eighteen or nineteen years old. My guess is that we'll soon know he was an Old Believer, that he had that name, too. Was a horrible scene."

I thought Cope was about to say something else, ask a question about the body maybe, but he didn't. Around us the café looked like any other place in a small Alaska town. A table of women crocheted together, laughing every once in a while, and a few couples talked quietly over their food. In the corner, I saw a lonely guy on a white MacBook laptop, pecking away at the keys. Seemed like a sight straight out of San Francisco for a moment. Everyone there pecked away incessantly at MacBooks in cafés. Writers all, I suspected—or just peckers who wanted to be.

Cope broke me out of it when he nodded at Martinez coming over. He stood up to shake his hand.

"BLT," Martinez said, setting a sandwich in a wicker basket down on the table in front of my seat. He and Cope did the introductions. Then Martinez said, "I'll leave you two to it." He pointed at an empty table by the counter. "I'll just be over there if you need me."

I lifted off the top piece of rich-looking wheat bread and approved of what I saw underneath: on top of some lean bacon sat lettuce and tomato so fresh it could have come right from Salinas. Sure, I wouldn't eat pork like this at home, but when in Rome…or in Homer, anyway. Maybe it was even from a bear.

I took a few bites and found it tasted as good as it looked.

Cope's face changed from friendly back to serious again, and he said, "You asked about his hand. Sure enough it had a nasty scar on the palm, just like you were saying." He pointed to my gauze and then made a vertical line. "Had to fingerprint him on more than one occasion, and he never liked it. Hated anyone touching him, making him do something. Often I needed a deputy to help me hold him or sometimes two. This boy, he had a kick something awful."

I put the sandwich down. "He ever hurt a woman?"

Cope shook it off. "Not in the time I knew him. But like I said, he was only around here for a short summer."

"You said you didn't like what happened. How did things end up?"

Cope frowned. "Town boys just run him off. Even some of my own men."

Martinez was finishing his sandwich and his calls on the other side of the café. I decided to let Cope talk himself out.

"Round about half a dozen times I arrest this asshole, I get sick of it. So I go to a few others in town, you know, some of my friends, and they took him outside the Down East one night, just a handful of them, and made it clear he wasn't wanted no more."

He turned, looked off out the window into the distance, then over the water to the west, toward where there wasn't anything to see.

He shrugged. "It's a small town. We take care of our own. Maybe I did wrong by him, not making any case of what they done, but there just wasn't room for him here, not with what he done to some of his sparring partners. Boy just didn't know when to quit. He didn't."

I pushed away my plate and it clinked against the salt and pepper shakers. I'd let Cope go on, taking things where he wanted, and he'd given me a lot.

"Do you know what all they did to him?"

With his bottom lip thrust out, Cope shook his head. "Nothing permanent, just roughed him up. You know, a good pounding. Like they was tenderizing the meat on a good old moose.

"Anyway, we didn't see him after. Was a Navy ship put into port around then, and I just figured he found his way on it, got his self out and away. We were better off."

"You think you'd recognize him now?"

He thought it over, looking around the café as he did. It occurred to me that this wholesome bakeshop, with women crocheting and great pastries, made an odd place for a small-town ex-cop to be spending his afternoons, but I didn't mention that. He probably wanted to be a writer, too.

"I might recognize him, but couldn't say for sure. Ten years a long time."

I took the composite sketch out of my briefcase, and as I did, I looked at my watch. The sketch artist would be meeting Alexandra at the restaurant on Sterling Highway about now, most likely drawing a boy who was dead. I had a few more questions about her village and their hand-cutting traditions, and if I was lucky, I might be able to catch her before they were done.

With the drawing of Andrews's description in my hands, I took another look at the face. It made me feel something: call it disgust, general unease, even a touch of fear. Any of these names, it was something in my gut, something that felt like my fear of heights set upside down. I turned the picture around and slid it across the table.

"Do you recognize this man as the boy you ran out of town ten years ago?"

He raised his finger, and I knew right away he'd take issue with how I'd said that, so I apologized. "I didn't mean it to come out like that," I said. "You were just doing your job, I know that."

He nodded and took the picture in his hands, turned it a little from side to side to get a few looks from different angles. "It could be him," he said. "Facial hair real different, but that happens to a man as he grows up. You know?"

I said I did.

"Boy did have a beard, though. He look different, what I'm saying, but I won't say this can't be his face. Ten years, a drawing from a sketch artist. This is Smitty's work, am I right?"

I nodded. In a town like this, there wouldn't be more than one sketch artist for the police, and he'd likely have the job for quite a while. I made a mental note to ask Billy Moose if Smitty was his name.

"Yeah. This looks just like his work." Cope put the drawing back down on the table, pushed it across to me. "Could be him," he said, nodding. "But the hat and the thick beard make it hard to tell. Plus, if you've seen enough of Smitty's work, they all start to blend together."

"What if I told you he had a cut vertically on his palm like you'd described about your Vitali Nikolaevsk?"

"That could make for a definite connection." His head bobbed in small movements. "Can't say I ever seen another cut like that in my time on the force."

"Except that now I have one." I raised my gauzed hand just enough for him to notice.

"Sure, that's true now. But I mean in my time, in people I run out of Homer or arrested or ever shook the hand of, that's the one time I seen a cut like that. Just that one."

Across the café, the table of women crocheting broke out into loud laughter, cackles and peals about something one of them had read off her phone.

As I was sliding the sketch off the table, I reached into my briefcase and pulled out Andrews's mug shot on instinct—trying to be thorough, I guess. I showed it to Cope.

"You ever seen this man?"

He laughed. "Sure as shit. Jason Andrews, a fucking loser if I ever knew one. Him?" He was shaking his head now. "That boy do just about anything you could imagine. Always looking to get himself a bad buck."

"We got this sketch off a description from Andrews. He cut my hand. Said this guy paid him four hundred dollars."

Cope whistled. "A fucking idiot. That boy is just plain dumb as deer shit." He shrugged. "But what can you do? No sense leads to no sense. Just like his father. Big drinkers, the both of them. But you catch him at something, he won't lie."

I stood up, slid both pictures back into my briefcase. It was closing in on three forty-five now, and I wanted to be sure we'd catch Alexandra before she went back into Nikolaevsk. No way Martinez or I would want to go back there again.

CHAPTER 32

We called the old restaurant—which turned out to be named just that: the Olde Restaurant—and caught Alexandra and Smitty as they were wrapping up. I got her on the line and asked her to wait, said I had a few more questions to ask. She agreed, though I could tell she didn't like it.

Old Billy Moose didn't get us there too fast either, since he drove only one particular way—however he wanted. Martinez kept glancing over at me, making hand gestures like *couldn't Billy speed this up a little*, and I can't say I disagreed.

I whispered, "Maybe the Homer police could have loaned us one of their cars."

He said, "*Commandeer* is the word for it. Next time that's what we do."

"Tell me what you found out about the water taxis."

His pad open, Martinez said, "Nada. Zero. I talked to every one of them and no one took over a kid of that description. However he got out there, it wasn't with one of the locals."

"So how'd he get there?"

"Exactly."

I stared out the window, trying to think it all through. The hike had done me some good, as had being outdoors, but I was getting a little too used to the scenery speeding by while I sat in a car. Billy had a habit of pointing out the occasional moose as he drove; he had an eye for it I couldn't believe. He picked out moose I would never have seen with binoculars. Just ticked them off like they were there in plain sight.

Still, after a while I had the feeling that when I'd seen one moose...Well, you get the idea.

In my head, I kept going back to the bloody scene on the trail. The images, the uselessness of it all. If this kid was really Vitali Nikolaevsk, what had he been doing out there? On a whim, I asked Billy how he'd feel about driving us out to Nikolaevsk if we needed to pay the old town a visit. He met my eyes in the rearview mirror.

"You sure? I mean, they don't much mind tourists out there, treat 'em to some samovar tea and all, but you types? Feds?" He shook his head and whistled. "No, ma'am. You types don't have no truck out there in they eyes. And they don't like you. So I'd drive you out for the tea, but you want otherwise, I got no need."

"Still, if we *had* to make a trip?"

He considered it for a moment. Then he checked his meter, which had been steadily ticking away all afternoon. It was coming up on $150, which was still nothing in the DC coffers.

"Yeah. I'd do it."

Martinez leaned toward me. "*Commandeer*," he whispered.

When we got to the restaurant, Niki's bike was parked out front. He stood tall on the porch as if he was tired of waiting. It was close to four thirty, and I could bet he was.

"Is your wife inside?" I asked him as I started up the stairs.

He nodded. I'd known the answer, and if I thought I'd get a better read on his attitude, or if I thought it had improved, I was mistaken.

Martinez came in with me again, and this time I pulled out a chair at Alexandra's table and offered it. When I insisted, he took the chair. I was going to need some additional opinions soon, besides my own.

We sat down across from Alexandra. The same mugs were on the table as before. I hoped with new coffee. Smitty the sketch artist was standing nearby, eager to show what he'd done. When he set it down on the table, I saw the wholesome-looking face of a young man. He had just started growing facial hair, and his beard had barely come in. Something looked mean or sinister, but I knew that was likely due to Alexandra's description more than anything else. And Cope was right, once you'd seen one of Smitty's drawings, you could see his touch in another. They did kind of look the same.

Whether this face was the one sheared off the body in the woods, I couldn't be sure. But there wasn't enough here to rule it out. The eye color matched—a soft, light blue that belied what I was starting to think of as a very bloody existence.

I asked Smitty if I could speak to him alone for a moment. Then I apologized to Alexandra for asking her to wait a little longer. She waved it off, but I could tell she wasn't happy.

From the look of Niki outside, I figured I had about fifteen minutes before he took her away physically, or the whole town of Old Believers came out in a search party.

Off to the side, I asked Smitty, "From this sketch, do you think you would recognize the skull type and shape of this man if you had to see his head without its skin?"

"Sure would." Smitty smiled. "Lady, I took the class down at Quan-tee-ko and everything. I been trained by the best. We studied skull types as a part of how to create faces and everything."

"Good. Because my partner's going to show you a few photos on my camera of what I think is this person without his face."

He looked at me to see if I was serious.

"Peeled off," I said.

"Sheee-it."

I called Martinez over with the camera, and he went with Smitty to the back. I didn't want Alexandra to have to see the pictures or know what had happened. Whether he'd been her friend or not, I wanted to spare her those sights.

I came back and apologized for a last time. "I really appreciate your waiting to talk," I said. "This means a lot to me and to this case."

"Is okay."

"I want to ask you about something that may have happened in Nikolaevsk about ten years ago. Is that all right? I know you were young, but if there's a chance you might remember, it'd be really helpful."

I was getting effusive and hoped it would help. I even took a mug of the oil-slick coffee and added cream. I'd eaten the rest of the BLT in the car on the way over, at Martinez's insistence, and my stomach was feeling up to the challenge.

Alexandra looked thoughtful for a few moments, a half minute perhaps, and then she spoke. "It is possible that I not remember so far back to then. I was only eight or nine. But Niki, he remember better." She started to get up, indicating toward him. "Is okay?"

"Really?" I wanted to jump up and shake her hand if she could get him to talk to me, but I stayed put. I didn't want to do anything more to put either of them off.

"I think maybe he help," she said.

She went out to the porch to her husband, and I half expected the two of them to go straight for his bike and ride off. I was even considering how much it'd cost extra to get Billy Moose to drive us on a chase. Not that he could catch anyone; the gray cab couldn't go more than thirty miles an hour.

When I saw Niki nod, listening to his wife, and his face go calm, I almost couldn't believe it. Then he was following her inside and sitting down across from me. I smiled and thanked them.

That was when Martinez came over to our table, and I could sense the tension picking up.

"Would you mind waiting outside?" I asked him. "I'm sorry, but—"

He took one look at Niki and didn't sit down. "Sure thing, boss," he said with a smile. "I'll just wait outside by the car."

Then he leaned down to me and whispered what Smitty thought: the skinned skull in the woods and the face he'd just sketched from Alexandra's description were the same person. "He's ninety-five percent it's the young Vitali Nikolaevsk."

"Thanks."

Martinez left us. As soon as he was gone, Niki seemed to settle in his seat.

Outside, I heard the start of a loud engine, which would be Smitty getting ready to drive back to Homer.

"I want to ask a few questions," I said. "About something that may have happened in Nikolaevsk maybe ten years ago."

Alexandra started explaining this to him in Russian, translating, and Niki raised his hand.

"I understand," he said. "I listen."

CHAPTER 33

"Alexandra told me about a boy from your village—Vitali—who recently did wrong and was asked to leave. Just a few weeks ago."

I watched them carefully as I spoke, worried I'd say the wrong thing.

"She also mentioned that Nina, the woman who I spoke to the other day in your village—"

Niki said, "She is elder."

Alexandra shifted in her seat, uncomfortable in her role between us.

I tried lowering my head to meet her eyes. "Nina. She's your leader?"

She nodded.

"I want to know who the leader was before her, or if there was a different person ten years ago?"

"Why you want to know about this? Our village?"

"I just spoke to one of the policemen in Homer. He's retired, but we talked about a summer ten years ago when a man from Nikolaevsk caused some trouble in Homer. They ran him out of town. But the thing is…" I raised my bandaged hand. "He had a cut on his hand similar to the one Nina gave Vitali. Remember, I told you I had a cut just the same, one that goes up and down?"

"Alexandra told you about cut?"

We both nodded, we women. I didn't want her to get in trouble, but what was done was done. I thought of showing them both the pictures of Vitali's hand mounted on a stick out in Kachemak State Park, but I'd told myself I wouldn't put them through that.

"He had a scar like this," I said, tracing my finger down my own palm along the bandage. "And now I have this cut, too. I'm trying to figure out what it means."

"It is punishment," Niki said.

"But why would one be across this way"—I showed them—"and another be up and down?"

Niki stopped to look at his fingers. Alexandra turned to him.

"That's really what I want to know: Why someone would have the vertical scar, and who is he? Do you remember someone—a man—getting punished like this about ten years ago?"

Finally, Niki raised and lowered his shoulders. "This I not know. This difference. It is punishment, both. Why one is up and other not?" He shrugged. "Nina make cut like this on Vitali to cause hurt when he work. All men in village must work. Vitali never forget his wrong if she cut him here." He motioned across his palm, and I could imagine how this scar would rub against the handle of an ax or a hoe for the rest of someone's days.

"Has anyone else ever gotten cut like this? By Nina or someone else?"

"I was young," Niki said. He turned up his hands like he was opening a book, revealing the thick calluses of days spent at hard labor. They were hands that spoke of a life among the elements, living off the land. They were hands that had earned their keep, had much to be proud of. He carried himself as though he knew this.

He started over. "I was young, so I not know so much. They don't say. These things, parents keep hidden from children. Things of shame. But I remember his screams."

Alexandra turned to face her husband. "Screams?"

I asked, "When they cut his hand?"

Niki pursed his lips. "No. In night, I remember his screams from my parents' house. My mother say he have demons. They keep him up, make him feel pains in his head."

"Demons? What kind of demons was she talking about?"

"I do not know. Only that he have." He raised his head again, shaking it in uncertainty as if to ask who could know anything about such things as the haunting of a person.

"He older than me. Old enough that I only see him in fields."

He stopped abruptly. I was still thinking about what these screams might sound like in the night of a village without street lamps, without electricity. Especially to a young child in winter nights that lasted weeks on end.

Niki continued. "He do bad things then. Fight with man over daughter." With his eyes closed, he added, "I am not sure. But he do wrong, worse than Vitali." His voice dropped to a whisper then. "He spill blood of man."

I waited for what he'd say next as though the restaurant around us had disappeared. Where it had been quiet before, now it seemed eerily absent.

"They make him leave. Cut his hand. Nina, she do this."

"His name?" I asked.

"After he leave, I hear his mother cry at night. Now *her* tears and cries replace his screams." He lowered his head, hiding his eyes.

"What was his name, Niki?"

"His name Ivan."

"Ivan," Alexandra repeated. "Yes. This name I have heard." She turned to her husband and said something in Russian. From the little I understood, he agreed with her. *Da. Da.*

"Vanya," she said. "We call Vanya."

She said more to her husband in Russian, but then he started to disagree. *Niet. Niet. Niet.*

He pounded his fist on the wood. My cup shook and some coffee spilled out.

Alexandra said, "He say you can't talk to Nina about why she cut. We cannot take you back to village."

"It's all right." I touched her hand. "Believe me, I understand."

Niki nodded, like this had all been decided before.

"What happened to Ivan?"

Niki pushed his lips out in a frown. "We know nothing outside of Nikolaevsk." He traced a box on the table with his finger. "This we not know. He leave. He gone."

I sat back in my chair. They appeared more at ease having told this story—to have it out. I wasn't sure if there was anything more for me to ask.

"I hear one thing," Alexandra told me. "They say he hurt a girl, a daughter of our village. He do wrong to her and then her father angry. Vanya, he cut him."

Niki nodded gravely, as if to admit this was a shame to their whole village. "Blood of man," he said.

"And blood of woman?"

Niki kept his head down, wouldn't meet my eyes. When I turned to Alexandra, she looked away. Very softly, so quiet that I could barely hear, she said, "Yes."

I let that hang in the air for a few moments, feeling like something had slammed into place. Then I tapped the table for one more question.

"Between then and now, only two people have been scarred like this? Cut on the hand? Just these two in the last ten years."

They both agreed without having to consider it.

"Yes," she said. "Absolute."

"One last thing." I took out the drawing from Andrews's interview and set it in front of Niki. "Is this Ivan? Could this be what he looks like now?"

He touched the bottom of the paper with his fingertips, careful not to dirty it with his hands. "Vanya," he said.

Alexandra glanced up from the picture. "Yes," she said. "He think yes."

"Maybe," Niki said, and then firmly, "*Da*. This Vanya. *This is Ivan.*"

CHAPTER 34

Martinez and I watched them ride off on Niki's bike.

"They were helpful?"

I turned back to the cab, ready to ride to the plane and get the hell out. No more Billy Moose, no more slow rides in taxis, no more blood in the woods; just make it through an hour in that plane and be back in Anchorage. My stomach tightened.

"They were helpful," I said.

"Linstrom called my cell while you were talking. He says it's important. To call him right away."

"Will do." I got into the back of the cab and told Billy Moose to take us to the Spit. When Martinez was in, Billy peeled out across the gravel shoulder and made a U-turn to head us back toward Homer. I was already getting out my phone.

I saw a red circle with the number four inside it displayed in the voice mail section. I called Linstrom, figuring I'd just get his bad news directly.

"About time you called in" was the first thing he said when he picked up.

"And hi to you, too."

"Owens is on his way down there," he said, "to look at the blood. Thought you'd want to know."

"Oh." It wasn't the information I'd been expecting, but it was good news. I needed Owens to give me everything he could from the scene out at Kachemak State Park.

"He's got his full report on Samantha Parker's apartment with him, too. I figured you'd want him to make a thorough analysis of the scene in the woods before any weather interferes."

"Yeah. That's perfect. How's he getting here?"

Linstrom laughed. "Driving. We can't all have the District of Columbia picking up our tabs."

I had to smile. "We're coming home. Back to Anchorage. I'll get his report when he has it."

"Sure. That works. I'll see you when you're back in Anchorage this time, okay?"

When I'd agreed, he hung up. I was still in the cab's backseat, dodging flapping fabric as we clunked along the highway.

"You know he likes you, right?"

"Yeah, Martinez. I remember you mentioning that."

"Well, he does. Just making sure you know. And Owens? He just wants to get in the middle, doesn't he? Or at least that's how it looks."

"We'll be in Homer soon," I said. "Then we fly back to Anchorage, and you don't mention any of this to anyone."

"Aye, aye, captain." When he saw my look, he got serious. "I mean, ma'am."

In the front seat, Billy Moose laughed. I was ready to get back to Anchorage, plane ride or not.

CHAPTER 35

Back in Anchorage, the next few days passed without much excitement. I got caught up on my report writing, read through as many of the old files from 2006 as I could, and sifted through the three new files—Parker's, Howard's, and the boy's—for anything I'd missed.

I spent extra time on conference calls to Bos and Withers, justifying my expenses thus far and giving them a loose version of my progress report for Senator Parker. Most of the facts and ideas I'd come up with about Nikolaevsk I left out in favor of vague suspicions about Alaskan locals and creepy truck drivers. Whatever the political situation between Alaska and Nikolaevsk, I didn't want anyone from DC mucking about in it, not if I wanted to keep any line of communication open with Alexandra and Niki.

I spent my nights by myself at the hotel, reading files. Linstrom was more than friendly around the office, and Owens stayed down in Homer for two days collecting evidence from the two scenes and the autopsies, documenting the various parts of bodies our killer or killers had left behind. We spoke on the phone briefly, and I promised to catch up over coffee when he was back in town.

"There's something extremely odd and disturbing about this case that we need to talk about," he said over the phone. When I pressed him for more on what he meant, he said it was "in the blood."

"Names," he told me, and that was enough for me to know he'd seen my name at Samantha Parker's and again at Kachemak. He had yet to add this to any of the reports, however, which meant he was willing to talk to me about it first.

Owens knew how hard I had to fight to stay on this case in '06, and we both knew if he made it public that this killer knew me, was even hunting me, someone up top would pull me off the case fast. They'd say they were doing it for my own protection, as if I needed someone to watch over me and make decisions about my safety.

Owens knew my history and stubborn streak better than anyone in Alaska or San Francisco; he knew it well enough that it ended our dating-hookup-sex ritual in '06. Whatever it was, it had lasted almost four months. Looking back on that, I couldn't blame him for getting fed up, but neither could I change who I was. Now he was covering for me, which couldn't last. I agreed to have coffee. At the very least, I owed him that.

On Thursday night, he was heading back up from Homer, and I sat in my hotel room alone, having brushed off another of Linstrom's invitations to dinner. I was trying to think it all through before I had to talk to Owens in the morning.

Sure, there were a couple of people in San Francisco I'd been on dates with in the past year, but nothing special. I'd traded a few more texts with Roberts and we'd talked on the phone; she cared enough to check in on me. But there was no guy in my life to call, no one I wanted to check in with from the road. In truth, Owens had been my last real boyfriend—and maybe I still wasn't comfortable calling him that.

In San Francisco everyone dated online, meeting strangers on OkCupid or Match. This didn't work for me. Either I did the wrong "winks" at the wrong guys or gave off the wrong sense of humor in the e-mails that followed. The few dates I went on were losers. Most guys in the city were either jock-head rich boys more in love with themselves than any woman they'd ever meet or FBI fanboys who asked too many questions about who I was.

At thirty-six, I should have been married with kids, loving a man, and living in the suburbs with a decent set of cars in a garage.

That had been the plan, anyway. But after the police academy and then law school, when the Bureau became an option that presented itself, I couldn't resist. Then everything became about proving myself, solving each case, doing superior work, and getting the job done every time out. All of this—it was like an addiction I couldn't break, didn't even want to. Nothing else mattered.

In the mirror above my hotel desk, I caught sight of my face, saw the same desire I'd always shown: the one-track determination to get to the bottom of things, spike a volleyball in somebody's face, or beat out my competitors for whatever was the new goal. Here I was, my takeout dinner pushed aside, hair pulled back into a tight bun, and a set of files open in front of me—murder cases all, each one grislier than the last. Here I was: Jess Harding, FBI agent and workaholic on a Thursday night. Bored and lonely in equal measures.

Out the window, I saw the light sky, and it made me feel as if life had more to offer. Always more to offer here in the Alaskan summer, more you could see and do in the course of a single day. The clock read ten thirty. In San Francisco and the rest of the Lower 48, it would be quiet and dark. Not here and not with the way I was feeling. Damned if I wanted to go right to bed and wake up to a breakfast of reckoning with Owens. He'd want to know two things: how I planned to keep myself from getting hurt when this Daylight Killer knew exactly who I was, and how long I expected him to keep that a secret from people in the Bureau who would want to protect me.

"By doing things right" was my answer to how I'd catch Ivan Nikolaevsk. And "forever" was how long I wanted him to hide the details about my name. Neither of which Owens would like.

I stood up and slipped on my jacket, tucked my cotton shirt back into my pants, and put on my dress boots. An agent I was and an agent I would be, but sometimes I had to get out and try to live.

CHAPTER 36

The Marriott in downtown Anchorage has one of the nicer bars in the city, if you're looking for fancy. If you're looking to have a drink and sit around with traveling businessmen and an occasional agent, that's the spot. But when I lived in Anchorage, my favorite spot was the F Street Station, right by the old Federal Building and National Archives—thank Christ we didn't still have offices in that wreck.

F Street Station was known for having a huge block of cheese at one corner of the bar for anyone to sample. When the Health Department found out about the lack of refrigeration and the block of cheese that lasted more than a week, they said to cut it out. In typical Alaskan fashion, the bar's response was to do something different. What they did was hang a sign right over the cheese block that announced, FOR DISPLAY PURPOSES ONLY. NOT FOR CONSUMPTION. Other than that, they left it the same as ever, kept on replacing the cheese when it got small, and folks kept on eating it, just as they always had. As far as anyone knew, no one had ever gotten sick, and the Board of Health no longer had a problem.

When I walked in from the Marriott, the cheese was on the bar, covered in a thin sheet of plastic wrap—and under the same sign. Now there was a huge bucket of candy next to it: everything from Tootsie Rolls to gum to Smarties and Starbursts. A regular Halloween dream.

What seemed different to me right away was the age of the people in the bar. As I ordered a Ketel One martini straight up with an olive, I felt like one of the older folks in the room. There had always been a good share of just-twenty-one types around, but now

I felt as though the average age of the people around me was *young*. Younger than me by enough to notice. Maybe I was just used to San Francisco bars, the kind of scene where everybody went out, at any age.

That, or maybe I was dressed like a Fed and felt like one, too.

I found a chair at the far corner of the bar and tried to keep my eyes off the television. With the array of Anchorage regulars around me, the likes of whom I was no longer used to seeing, it wasn't hard.

"You new around here?" someone asked.

I turned to see a man just a little older than me, in good shape but with creases around his eyes—from smiling, I thought, not from age. He wasn't bad looking either. His hair had just a touch of gray.

"That easy to tell?" We laughed. "Truth is I couldn't sleep."

He glanced around, waiting to see if I'd come in by myself. "Why sleep on a night like this? Light out and full of sun? Alaskan summer was made for people to enjoy."

I toasted to that with him, drank down a good slug of the cold, thin vodka. It tasted right.

"You don't mind me asking, what happened to your hand?"

"Only a burn." I waved it off. "I forgot how good the summers can be here. But I don't know how I could've." He slid his chair closer. No one seemed to be paying attention.

"How long did you live here?"

I told him a story: about my year of working in the Anchorage office of a big trade conglomerate based out of San Francisco and how I'd been relocated to the main office and worked there for a few years since. He'd lived in Anchorage all his life, ran a contracting firm that got some business from the pipeline folks. He made a good living and didn't like Sarah Palin. That seemed good enough to me.

"You ever eat that cheese?" I nodded in the direction of the big block of yellow cheddar.

He bowed his head, sheepish. "I have, but I'm not proud."

"Looks like a good block. More than anything, I just want to know how it tastes."

He stood up and pushed in his stool. "It's *good*," he said. "Come on. You have to try now."

I protested as best I could, but Trent wouldn't take no for an answer. That was his name, Trent. Trent Voight, the nice guy from Anchorage. I downed the rest of my martini, ate the olive for fortification, and let him lead me around the bar.

An older guy was carving off a piece for himself, and we had to wait. A couple of women were sifting through the candy bucket and lining up Tootsie Rolls of various colors on the bar. They said something to Trent, and it turned out he knew them. He introduced me, and everyone was all smiles. Now it didn't seem that I was the oldest person in here. I felt okay; no one even stared as I made my move on the cheese.

Trent put the slicer in my hand, and I carved off a big piece. Then he handed me a Ritz cracker, and I ate it with the cheese. Now I was officially in violation of the Board of Health. I didn't care.

"Display purposes only, my ass," Trent said. He laughed, and the women with the candy did, too. I found myself laughing through the cracker, spitting out crumbs, wondering how the single martini had gotten to me so fast.

Soon Trent put another martini in front of me, and I wanted a cigarette. It had been a while since I'd smoked, not since the last of my good dates in San Francisco. *That* was a long time.

I was enjoying myself. For the first time in a while I didn't feel like an agent or that I needed to act a certain way. I was just Jess Harding, the girl from western Massachusetts.

Trent and I closed the place. Light out or not, the law said bars had to close at two in the morning and they stuck to it, despite how they responded to the Board of Health about cheese. I wasn't drunk, but I was happy. Breakfast with Owens had slipped my mind, and if I had thought about it then, I'd have been ready to let him tell anyone he wanted about the Daylight Killer knowing my name and where I used to live. Let the higher-ups have that info and do what they wanted with it. I was letting go. It was time. Maybe protecting me wasn't such a bad thought. I didn't need to be a hard-ass all the time.

Sometimes just being human was all right, I hoped.

Trent looked good in his khaki trousers, and I didn't mind that at all. I cupped his backside with my good left hand as he walked me back to my hotel, and his eyes popped open in surprise. That made me want to kiss him. I pushed him backward into a small alley, stood him against the wall and put my mouth against his. His lips were sweet and soft. I wanted him to come back to my hotel room.

I whispered against his face, "Maybe taking everything so seriously isn't always the best way to be."

"Maybe not," he said.

"Really?"

He nodded slowly and kissed me again. I felt his hand along my back, sweeping up my spine and over my shoulder to rub the cords at the base of my neck. His fingers tickled. I liked that.

"You're sweet," I said.

He smiled against my lips and touched his forehead to mine. I laughed.

"Can I take you home?"

I squeezed his hip against me.

"I think you better."

That was when a rough voice broke into our small, comfortable world. "You folks spare a quarter?"

Trent absently handed the guy some change.

"Thanks. Now how about twenty dollars, you fuck?"

We both stopped and looked. My heart dropped out of my chest. The man had a scarf over the lower half of his face, but I knew.

It was *him*.

That was when Ivan Nikolaevsk pulled Trent away from me and threw him against a wall. He plunged a knife into Trent's stomach before I could react, and then he ripped it up toward his sternum. Trent's chest made a sound like so many tubes and organs sliding together. He called out.

I couldn't believe what I was seeing, or how fast everything had changed. My heart jumped a beat; I reached around to the small of my back for my gun, where I usually kept it, and it wasn't there. I was trying to take a night off. This was supposed to be me as a human—a normal woman.

I steadied myself against the wall, pushing off it with my bad hand. A jolt of pain snapped through me. I kicked Ivan in the side of his leg, aiming for the back of his knee, but missed. My foot bounced off his thigh.

Ivan pushed Trent's right hand up on the wall and stabbed his knife into it hard enough that it must have gone clear through. He was tall, standing over Trent.

"See this, Harding?"

He turned to me, pulling the scarf away to show his face. I saw the Cyrillic tattoo on his neck and how much he looked like the picture Smitty had done. Then I knew him, too, remembered his face and him helping me down from the old-timer's truck that night. He'd trimmed his beard since then, but the eyes were unmistakable: pale blue and wild, full of mischief and pain.

"Fuck you!" I kicked him in the shin as a follow-up, a straight-on blast to see how he liked that. Then I came back higher with a knee to his groin and the toe of my boot into his kidney as soon as he doubled up. With that, he pulled back and cringed. His knife was still in Trent's hand, and he had no weapon, but I needed to move fast—he outweighed me by at least a hundred pounds.

His head was right in front of me because he'd doubled up after the shot to his kidney, so I measured it and put all I had into one clean shot with an open hand to his temple. It rocked him; he went down and rolled. But I'd forgotten about my right hand for a moment, the cut Andrews gave me, and now I saw red from the pain. Of course I'd hit him with my open palm. Of course.

Ivan rolled up onto his hands and knees and met my eyes. He touched his lip and saw blood on his finger. He smiled.

I wrenched the knife out of Trent's hand and Trent crumpled to the ground.

CHAPTER 37

"See this?"

The Daylight Killer held out his right hand, showing me his palm and the cut that ran down it, the thick scar like the one I would have some day from the damage Andrews had done. I'd pay whatever it took to get the best plastic surgeon and make that scar disappear. No way was I going to carry this guy's mark as a reminder for the rest of my life.

I kicked up at his face like it was a soccer ball. He flinched, tucked into his shoulders, but still my foot glanced off the top of his skull. I tried the knife, but he blocked my hand and knocked it to the ground. I followed with a jab to the space between his shoulder and face, into the soft of his neck. He fell back into the wall, coughing. Behind me, I heard Trent make an awful sound. He groaned like a gutted animal, which he was, and I knew his breaths were numbered.

Now Ivan smiled at me again, licking blood from his lips as though he enjoyed the taste—as if he wanted me to beat him for everything because it turned him on. I didn't care. This was my guy, and I was happy to oblige.

I stepped into it and kicked him in the ribs, then the stomach, trying to launch him off the ground, break something, rip him open. I saw red.

My boot connected, and I felt something give, but then he caught my leg at the ankle, held my foot against his stomach and rolled over, dropping me onto my ass.

"Fuck you!"

From my back, I kicked wildly at him with my other leg until he let go of my foot. I slipped away, crawled back toward the wall where Trent had fallen.

Trent reached for my shoulder. "Help me, Jess," he said. I could feel his breath hot against my neck, hear the desperation in his voice. He coughed, and I felt blood spatter my cheek.

I fumbled for my cell and found it as Ivan worked to stand. He still smiled, wiping blood off his mouth with the back of his wrist. Now his smile looked broken, harmed but still full of menace.

I dialed 9-1-1 as fast as I could.

"Fuck you, you sick fuck!"

Ivan stepped forward onto one knee and then onto his feet. I tried to scramble up, but Trent held me down, clawing at me to help him.

Ivan showed me his right palm again, his cut. "We are same now, you and me."

He barely had an accent like Niki and Alexandra; he almost sounded like anyone else, except his voice was hoarse and raspy and full of hate. He licked his palm and showed me the blood on his old cut.

"Just like you," he said.

My right hand hurt. I looked and saw blood staining the gauze.

I said, "Your name is Ivan. You came from Nikolaevsk. And I'm going to put you away."

He shook his head. Now he was standing over me. I heard the 9-1-1 dispatcher on the other end of my phone and yelled that I needed assistance in the alley off F Street between Fifth and Sixth.

Ivan kicked the phone out of my hand, and it skidded up the alley, spinning away.

"Fuck you." I pushed myself up using the wall, breaking free of Trent's grip to stand before Ivan. "I'm going to kill you," I told him.

His smile widened and his eyebrows slid up his forehead. In a deep voice, he said, "Are you, though? Isn't that against your job?"

I stood between Ivan and Trent. "I don't care."

"What if I get you first, Jessica?" I hated the sound of him saying my name. He slipped a bigger hunting knife out of his coat, wove it through the air, catching what light there was on the dim street.

"Now you know me," he said. "And you know how well I kill." He nodded at Trent. "My next victim will be a twenty-two-year-old blonde girl. Or maybe it will be you." He smiled. Then he stepped back and broke into a run out the alley and onto F Street, calling behind him that he would see me again as he made the turn.

I slid down to my knees, pulled at Trent's legs to drag him away from the wall so he could lie flat. The ground was soaked in his blood. He moved like he was in pieces, his chest rattling dully from inside. His intestines, his stomach, and his guts in general had slipped out of him into his lap. When I had him flat, some of it slid onto the ground. The blood coming out of him looked black. Sirens called in the distance, and I hoped one of them would be an ambulance.

Trent's eyes were wide, white, looking up at me in horror. He'd passed into a state of shock. Probably better for him that way. I held his hand, telling him everything would be all right.

I knew it was a lie.

CHAPTER 38

Linstrom was the first from the Bureau to meet me at the hospital. He came straight from bed to meet me in the waiting room. The doctors were doing what they could for Trent, but I knew it wouldn't be long until they came out and told me it was all over.

I was using my good hand to prop up my head, resting my elbow on my knee, and saw Linstrom's feet out of the corner of my eye. I heard him sit down in the next chair.

"We need to get you out of those pants," he said. "Those look like you could wring them out to give blood."

I didn't answer. He said, "We'll need to get you a tox screen, you know. Legally speaking."

I held out my forearm to let him go ahead and take the blood.

"Not right away, Jess. Just saying."

He put his arm around my shoulders, and I let out a sigh that I didn't know I'd been holding. I was doing everything I could to keep from crying.

"This was our guy?" he asked.

"Our guy."

"Wow. Fuck."

"Tell me again."

"He must have been watching you."

Between my feet, horrible white and black linoleum tiles shone painfully at my face, reflecting the fluorescents. "I tried to take a night off to unwind. I had a drink. I met this man."

"You—" Linstrom started and stopped.

I knew he wanted to say something about how I should have taken the night to come to his place and do something safe, something *with him*, but he stopped himself. I was grateful for that.

"You're right," I said. "I know."

"Or even with Owens."

I let that one hang in the air. "There's nothing with Owens," I said. "I'm just a girl away from home, out here by myself."

Linstrom pulled me closer to him. For the first time in what seemed like a long while, I let someone hold me. I closed my eyes.

When I opened them, the doctors were there and Linstrom was helping me to stand up. They were telling me what I'd known to be true, that this man who had been kind to me for only a short time and didn't deserve any violence against him was now dead. He had a daughter, it turned out, and I volunteered to be the one to tell her. I owed him that.

The night made for a long one, even if it didn't get dark; the hospital's fluorescents made it that so much worse. Something about sitting under those lights for an extended period, especially in the small hours, can make any bad situation worse.

The next day the higher-ups in the Bureau held a long meeting, one that included Linstrom and even Owens. I wasn't asked to come. Owens told them what he had known all along—that our Daylight Killer was targeting Samantha Parker because she had an apartment like mine. My own old place was inhabited by an old Vietnam vet, a burly man who hardly fit the profile of someone the Daylight Killer liked to slaughter.

They made a decision based on what they all thought was "the best thing for my own good," as they told me later, and I didn't fight it. My fighting for this case was over. Maybe Ivan had gotten to me, or maybe I just knew him too well—more than I ever wanted to. I needed a break.

I prepared a full report about Nikolaevsk, and Ivan, and both Vitali stories. I briefed Martinez and his new partner, who were to succeed me on the case. Martinez was taking the whole thing hard—what happened to Trent, and me going home—but I told him to hang in there. He was a good man, and he'd make a good agent. It was a strange coincidence that the Daylight Killer case had been a first for each of us, but I hoped he'd wrap up his time with it better than I had.

I told him Ivan was going after a blonde next, a young woman twenty-two years old. He could do it anywhere in the state, though, so that wasn't much of a lead to go on.

I called Bos and Withers and told them everything I had. They sounded more disappointed that I wouldn't be in Alaska to eat any more of the good fish than about the case going to somebody else.

Bos said, "We were just thinking about our next trip back and where we'd like to eat."

I apologized as best I could.

Then I went back to my hotel and packed. The clothes from Trent's death had been cataloged and put into evidence and that was fine; I never wanted to see them again. I was back to my gray pants suit, now back from the cleaners, and that would be more than okay.

Owens and I never had our coffee.

Linstrom picked me up the next afternoon to take me to the airport. In the car, we were quiet.

Finally, he said, "I'm sorry about all this. I really am. I know you're a great agent, Jess."

I thanked him with a nod. Maybe he saw it, and maybe he didn't.

"I *know* him now," I said. "I *know* this guy. Maybe even too well."

We were on L Street, where it turns into Minnesota, the closest thing to a real divided highway in the whole of the big, great state.

"But maybe he knows you, too. And that's definitely not how it's supposed to work. He's been *following* you, for Christ's sake."

"Why?" I asked. "Why do you think he took an interest in me?"

"You were hunting him, Jess. Look at the profile. This guy's a pure predator, looking to be the top of the chain. He's the hunter, and he doesn't like to be the hunted. Somehow you became another alpha, a threatening one."

"Maybe. Maybe that's the case."

He looked over at me, and I could almost feel his eyes along my skirt. "Plus, you're a woman. You fit his profile, even. These aren't good things."

I sat still. When I got back to San Francisco, I'd have a full week off to recover and recuperate. I was ready to take that time. Roberts knew I was coming back, and she'd volunteered to pick me up at the airport, but I dreaded filling her in on the most recent news.

"You guys watch him," I said as I was getting out of the car. "Watch for him everywhere. When he goes after someone, another woman, get him and stop him. I don't care what it takes."

Linstrom got out and brought my luggage around from the trunk. "We will, Jess. I promise."

He opened his arms and I moved into them; he wanted to hold me, and I let him—it felt good. Then I held him in return, squeezed him to me because he really was a good man. That was something every good woman sometimes needs, no matter what we may think.

"Thank you," I said. "For everything."

"No problem."

I held onto him and waited for his eyes to meet mine. When they did, I said, "No, really, Linstrom—Oscar. I want to thank you. You've helped me a lot here. I know I can trust you."

He nodded and stepped back toward the car. Now he looked a little bashful. "I'd have done it," he said and stopped. He said, "I would do even more if I had it to do over again."

"Thanks." I squeezed his hand and turned to go my separate way. I went into the airport to catch my plane—back to San Francisco.

PART II
SAN FRANCISCO

CHAPTER 39

Back in the city, I felt surprised every night when I looked up at the night sky and saw darkness. It disappointed me; it felt strange, like some element of magic I'd gotten used to in Alaska had gone away.

Every day I read the papers and checked my e-mail for something new from Anchorage, looking for a murder, a bust, anything related to the Daylight Killer. The white nights summer still had six weeks left, so I knew he couldn't wait long.

I pictured Ivan out there now, in the present, instead of just seeing pictures of what he had done in the past. Now it was more than just the images of the horrors and the deaths; now I imagined what he would do and whom he would do it to. I read up on the bars I thought he might try and placed calls to their bartenders, pleading with them to ask any young blonde women they saw to watch out.

Up in the Great Land, Linstrom, Martinez, and the other agents canvassed Anchorage with pictures of Ivan, Smitty's sketch now improved by my own testimony and what details I could add. They had a face that looked a lot like him, and now they even had a name. They spread out from Anchorage, casting a wider and wider net.

I had dinner with Roberts a few times in my first week back, trying to explain what had happened up there and why I'd gotten released to come right back. It wasn't a story I felt like telling, but she kind of wheedled it out of me. She had that way. Still, there wasn't much she could do to help me get over how I felt about Trent and even less to help me in assisting the investigation up north. She had her own problems with cases, a family who kept her running home to Oakland to see her husband and daughters, and what else could she really do?

So I watched the news and waited, read my e-mails, and researched the best plastic surgeons in California, looking for a topflight hand man or woman who could help me erase the scar that was my constant reminder of Ivan Nikolaevsk. I looked and watched and waited.

And nothing. Then one day, on a Friday, it fell right into my lap.

I was on a case watching a drug ring out of North Beach, trying to get leads on their supply by tracking the money. Then, over lunch, I saw e-mails about a murder case in the Mission, and I knew I had to get a look.

A twenty-two-year-old blonde girl had been killed. The details and facts weren't exactly the same—no barbed wire here and definitely no white nights—but I knew. He had come to California for me. I could hear him out there, almost as if he was saying my name.

Harding. Jess Harding.

I heard it just as clearly as when I first landed in Anchorage and saw Samantha Parker's apartment.

Jess Harding, it said, *I've come to San Francisco for you.*

He was out there looking for me. Only now something was different, something inside me. Now, instead of feeling a chill, I felt my blood racing; I wanted nothing more than to work this case. I wanted him. Seeing the e-mails, I felt a rush and knew what it felt like to hunt a wild grizzly. I wanted Ivan, wanted him dead or behind bars, more than I'd ever wanted anything else.

He was my man, and this was my case. *He was mine.*

I went to the brass and parlayed my successful record in San Francisco and my background gathering evidence on the Daylight Killer murders to get them to transfer me onto the case. I was given permission to look into it and see what I could find. Not free rein.

But still, no one wanted to stop me, and no one in the San Francisco office even suspected that they should try.

I felt a heightened awareness as I drove over to the Mission; I saw every pedestrian on the streets, noticed license plates, drivers in their cars. I saw everyone's face and cataloged them all.

On Twenty-Fifth Street, I parked and started toward where the dead woman had lived. I felt Ivan watching me. Only now, strangely, I liked this sense of being watched.

He was out there, just beyond my vision, barely out of sight, and the world was painted differently. He and I were the only ones who could see it.

I didn't want a partner or anyone else to get in my way.

The victim was a girl named Stephanie Harvey, a nurse at the Kaiser Permanente on Divisadero. When I got to her apartment, I asked all the police officers at the scene to leave me alone so I could experience the scene by myself, with no one watching.

After they left, I stood in her living room, my eyes closed, breathing in and out as deeply as I could. I could smell his smell; I knew he had been there.

He was in my city now, hunting me.

And I was hunting him.

CHAPTER 40

Like many other city dwellings, Stephanie Harvey's Mission apartment was small. She didn't make enough to afford one of the new condos in a remodeled building, so she found herself in an old house turned into apartments that needed new paint jobs and fresh supports for the warped floors. Her living room was small and full of cheap furniture from IKEA.

She had been struck on the head with something blunt, something they had yet to identify. But it made the same shallow dent that I'd seen in his work up north. I knew it was Ivan.

In the kitchen the SFPD detectives had found just two words written in blood: *dirty bomb.* Those were enough to bring the FBI in under the counterterrorism umbrella. He would have known that, of course, and somewhere, I bet, he'd smile when he knew I saw this. Of course I recognized the handwriting—and the fact that it was in blood.

The scene was like putting two and two together to solve a puzzle only he and I knew existed. It was what I saw in the bedroom, though, and the way he'd left her body that helped me understand his meaning. He had pushed beyond the carnage that had marked the crime scenes in 2006. Back then, it was just a kill—the blood, the barbed wire, the writing. Now he was obsessed with hands.

There was no barbed wire this time—too cliché at this point, I supposed, or too likely to trip particulars within our database that would match this up with the cases in Alaska. No, all of this was strictly for me. He had slashed both of her wrists horizontally, the way that doesn't work in suicides, and then slashed her palms vertically the way ours had been. But he didn't stop there. He'd stripped off all her clothes and—though the cause of death would later be identified as the blunt trauma to the head—he'd cut open her side like Adina Howard's in Homer a few weeks back.

As I looked closer, though, I could see it wasn't like Howard's cut—none of the carnage and mess that the hooking had done there. It was much more like Tina Bruce's cut from '06, as though he wanted me to see his handiwork again, know how he'd done it, and see the difference from this new Vitali's work. Of course it was cleaner. Of course I understood.

Vitali had been a copycat, and Ivan had made him pay.

I stepped back and shook my head, trying to clear it. I remembered the word in the woods next to Vitali: *fake*.

Suddenly I felt a chill at being alone in the apartment and reminded myself I had to be careful. I knew the officers were still waiting downstairs, and Ivan couldn't have been waiting in a closet all this time—they'd searched the place—but still I rushed to the living room and opened the door to the hall. There I saw an officer in blue, one of San Francisco's finest, and we exchanged nods.

"Thanks for waiting," I said. "I'll just be a few more minutes."

"Take your time."

I walked back through the living room and the kitchen, double-checking for anything I had missed. Then, when that didn't yield anything, I returned to the bedroom. Stephanie Harvey was laid out on her own bed, over the spread that had been perfectly tucked in before she was dropped onto it. From the tidiness of the rest of the apartment, everything in its place, I could see she was the type to make the bed every morning as soon as she got up. Fastidious. Maybe that was how Ivan liked them. Or maybe there was no pattern at all. Just young women he'd met somewhere in a bar.

I checked the small of my back for my weapon and drew it. Two nice things I liked about my Glock: you don't have to worry about a safety, and you don't have a hammer getting caught on anything. With one in the chamber at all times, it's ready to go. I felt its power but still knew I was very much alone.

Was I getting paranoid? I didn't know. Alone in an empty apartment with my gun drawn, the chill remained, and I had to wonder.

After a last look at Stephanie Harvey, especially her hands and palms, I put my weapon away and slipped out of the apartment, patting the uniform on his shoulder as I left.

Back in my car, I sat thinking, knowing there wouldn't be another killing in Alaska. Linstrom and Martinez and whoever else was waiting there could pack up and go home.

No, Ivan was here now, visiting my city. Maybe that would put the two of us on even ground. But I still needed backup. Someone I could trust, who knew what we were up against. My first thought was Roberts, but as the lead on the North Beach operation, she had too much on her plate.

I needed someone armed, aware of the case, and loyal. Someone who would protect me but not think I needed protection of the universal and departmental kind. I needed someone who'd be willing to bend the rules for me.

Martinez was too new, too green. Owens wasn't used to being armed, wouldn't be good in a pinch—after all, his forte was after-the-fact examinations—and I didn't know how far I could trust him.

Other than Roberts, my fellow agents in the city were good and many of them admired the work I'd done, but their friendship was different from friendship in Alaska. I'd been in the Anchorage office for less than two years and in San Francisco for five, but going back up there reminded me what good friends are, the real difference between casual relationships and people you would go to hell for. I didn't have many of those in San Francisco. Sure, everyone smiled and acted friendly and loved talking about making plans, but whether it actually came off was a whole other story. Real do-or-die friendship, someone you could count on? In Alaska that amounted to something different. Blame the weather, the elements, the harsh winters. People knew you couldn't survive all on your own and that meant something. It changed the way you saw others and treated them as friends.

Also, no one down here had any idea what we'd be up against.

It all meant Oscar Linstrom was my only man for the job.

I drove back to the Bureau and called him from the parking lot on my cell. He answered right away.

I said, "It's me," and he knew it all right then.

"Are you all right?"

"Yeah. I'm fine."

"He's there, isn't he?"

I adjusted the vent, turned the air-conditioning on my face. I suddenly felt flushed.

"I think he is."

"We've had nothing up here. Not a thing."

I wondered for a moment if I could really trust him, but then I just said it: "I've got a situation here I could use a friend on."

"Name it."

"No, I mean a real friend. This could go way outside the lines."

"Hang on." I could hear him on the other end: closing a door or sitting down, or just making sure no one else was around. "Tell me what you need. I've got ten vacation days saved, and they're all yours."

"I need a tail down here. Someone to watch my back."

"It's him? You're sure?"

I hesitated, but only for a moment. "He's here."

"You sure you don't want—"

"No."

"Okay. We can talk about this more when I get down there."

"No, we can't."

He paused then, and after a moment I could hear him sigh. A plane flew overhead, trekking from SFO to some point north or west of here. I watched it cut a white line across the sky. I let out my breath.

Linstrom said, "I'm on my way."

CHAPTER 41

For the rest of the afternoon I sat in my cubicle on the fourth floor. I drank my coffee like everyone else, searched the web, pretended I was doing research about Stephanie Harvey, and instead researched the Daylight Killer, looking over my files from 2006 again and trying to put together as much as I could about my man.

Who was Ivan Nikolaevsk? That was my main question. And where had he been for the five years from 2001 to 2006 and then again from 2006 to 2011?

I started looking at birth records for anyone with the last name Nikolaevsk. There wasn't much to find. The Old Believers were unlikely to venture into Homer or to a traditional hospital to deliver their babies. I thought of Nina sitting on her porch and wondered if she wouldn't be the one to deliver the town's children. A midwife as powerful as any man: I could see it.

The Old Believers wouldn't have birth certificates or even Social Security cards—anything that identified them or put them on the grid. I wondered if Niki even had a license to drive his motorcycle. How could he not? But I could see it.

I called the Homer police and asked for a way to reach Officer Cope. The dispatcher gave me a phone number, but before I hung up, I asked if she could pull a file for me: anything on an Ivan or Vitali Nikolaevsk.

"Oh, yeah," the dispatcher said. "You mean that boy just killed up Kachemak? Nasty business that was. Had to bust tail all over the county to get an ID on him."

She told me about Smitty reporting in on the sketch from Alexandra and how someone had to go out and show the picture around, ask the Old Believers if they could identify the face. Sure enough, they did it, grudgingly.

"Of course nothing come back from the fingerprints or the dental work. You know those old Russians don't go in for nothing like that."

"No?"

"Nope. None of it."

She'd confirmed what I thought. I asked her for this new Vitali file but also anything she could find from before 2011. She said she'd get back to me in a couple of hours.

"Old file system here," she said. "Most is still in file cabinets. I'll have to go look through 'em by hand."

"Sure," I said, "While you're at it, pull anything for me that you have on *anyone* with the last name of Nikolaevsk."

"Will do," she said. And she was gone.

I called Cope and left a message. He still had an answering machine, not voice mail. I could tell by the extended beep of the machine playing through its tape. No mechanized efficiency. No cell phone.

I asked him to call and left my number. I wanted to know how he'd been able to ID Vitali Nikolaevsk way back in 2001, if he'd had a driver's license or any formal identification. I wished him well before I hung up, told him to say hello to the women crocheting.

When that was done, I sat at my desk. The clock read four thirty, and I planned to stay right where I was until eight. At least eight—until I knew Linstrom was in the city, and I had a chance to talk with him.

While I waited, I looked through my old files. That was when something struck me as wrong; I knew something bad had happened to Cope. No way he had that many messages or calls in a day. No way it filled up his machine and left that long a playback beep.

I picked up the phone and called the Homer police back right away. I got the same dispatcher. She was quick to tell me she'd start looking through the files for what I needed "as soon as this damn phone stops ringing."

"I'm worried about Officer Cope."

"You try him at the Two Sisters?"

I confessed I hadn't, and she suggested I try him there. "I'll do it, but will you just send a car over to his house to check on him? I have a hunch that he's not okay."

"A hunch?" She sighed. "Yeah, I'll see if someone's over there in the area." She didn't sound concerned.

I looked up the café online, found its phone number, and called. When a girl answered, I asked if Officer Cope was around.

"Sure enough. I'm looking at him right now."

I felt a mix of relief and embarrassment. Now at least one person up there thought I was crazy. Or one more.

After a minute I heard, "Cope here."

"It's Agent Harding. We spoke last week about Vitali Nikolaevsk?"

"Ayyuh. The *old* Vitali Nikolaevsk. Not the dead one. He's younger. How about *that* twist to our story?"

"Right. Yes, the older one. From 2001. I wanted to know how you identified him, what kind of paperwork he had, being from Nikolaevsk and all."

He coughed. "Far as I can remember, he told us his name, and that was all we had. These people aren't even American citizens, you know. Just some cult of nut jobs."

I started to say something, but he cut in again. "I mean, they *might* be citizens, but they've got no paperwork. Not these nuts."

"No driver's license?" I made a note on my pad. If he'd been in the DMV, that would make things too easy.

"Who knows what they've got going on up there in Old Believer Town? Some kind of system, I guess, but not one I know about."

I thanked him, asked him if he'd mind putting a quick call in to the police department—to let them know he was all right.

"Why would I do that?"

I explained that I'd had a bit of a panic—maybe I was paranoid—but I'd just called to say I thought he was in trouble.

"Feds," he said, "Always expecting the worst." He coughed. "Sorry. I mean that in the best possible way."

"No offense taken," I said. "And if you'll call dispatch and check in, I'll owe you one on top of that."

He said he would, and I thanked him.

When we hung up, I had one dominant thought: maybe I *was* getting paranoid. But maybe, I reasoned, it was for my own good.

CHAPTER 42

I searched the military and DMV records in Alaska for a Vitali Nikolaevsk who first registered back around 2000 or 2001. Why? Just to do it, I guess.

Sure enough, no Vitali Nikolaevsk was on file with any of them. Not an Ivan or a Vanya either.

Then I had a stroke of brilliance: if he was used to being named for the place he was from, maybe he'd stick with that pattern. I tried the DMV records for an Ivan or a Vitali Homer. Then I hit it: one Ivan Homer had passed the driver's test in 2001 and gotten a license. An old picture of him showed up on the file. When the license expired four years later, it was never renewed. Ivan Homer had never received a parking ticket, registered a car, or been pulled over for any violation, not even speeding.

I blew up the picture of Ivan Homer from the license. It was him.

I printed it out and tacked it up on the wall of my cube next to the sketch done by Smitty. Ten years of aging but the faces were the same man.

"Nice mug shots there, Harding."

An agent leaned into my cubicle, staring at the pictures. I couldn't remember his name—Chris and Jeff were the two options I thought of, and he *looked* like a Jeff, but I wasn't sure.

"We're going out for a few drinks. Want to join us?" He tilted his head toward a few others milling around the printer at the end of my row.

Where was Roberts to shield me from unwanted socializing? Not here when I needed her.

"I'm good," I said. "Lots of work to catch up on. Had what looks like a terrorist murder this morning in the Mission. So…"

I let it trail off at that.

"Oh, wow. Yeah, work on that one for *sure*, Harding." He knocked on the wall of my cube. Why he did this now instead of when he first arrived, I had no idea. "But don't forget that it's Friday, okay? If you want to meet up after, we'll be over at Harrington's."

"Got it." I thanked him, and he was gone.

The pictures were still the same. The beard had changed and the face aged, but the man was there in both. I could see the hate in his eyes.

I'd seen that hate first-person now, what had spooked Willy R. Nelson, caused fights in Homer in 2001, and terrorized most of the Kenai Peninsula clear up to Anchorage in 2006. The hate that showed up only in the summer during white nights and only every five years.

Why?

It was the hate that had killed poor Trent. I closed my eyes and focused on my breath for a few beats. Trent should never have died; I never should have allowed myself to be followed like that, stalked, and for it to affect a civilian. It was all on me. My fault.

I tried putting it all out of my head, stood up to walk around the floor. I did my best thinking while walking, as did many of the agents, and so it wasn't a strange occurrence for some of us to get our best leads and insights while hanging around the water cooler. Some joked that was why we had it.

I went through our military databases, looking for a Vitali or an Ivan Homer. Sure enough, an Ivan Homer had joined the navy in Homer at the end of summer 2001. He'd joined up on a boat and done duty patrolling the Bering Sea, through the Strait and up around Russia, through the rest of that year. Then, in early 2002, he went missing.

That was it: a final entry of AWOL in Russian territory. No further details.

I thought back to how this fucker had wielded a knife, what he did to Trent. Poor Trent. There was definitely significant military training there. More than he could get on a half-year stint aboard a navy boat in peacetime.

This was about the time that we invaded Afghanistan and Iraq. Who knew where Ivan had gone off to? Sure, Russia was big, but if he could get to the other side of it, he wouldn't be that far from Iraq or Afghanistan.

I had to laugh. Saying one side of Russia to the other wasn't far was like saying I wasn't that far from Nova Scotia. Or Alaska, for that matter. What was a few thousand miles between conflicts?

Maybe he joined up with the Russian army after he deserted from our navy?

If I knew anything, it was that I didn't know much.

When Linstrom finally called, it was close to ten thirty.

"I'm here," he said. "Just got to SFO."

"Thank Christ. I mean, thank you, Oscar."

"It's okay. I told them my sister was having a medical emergency and that I needed at least a week to take care of her. They didn't mind. Even the DC guys have lost interest in Samantha Parker. After the big funeral, her father sort of went back to business as usual."

"Go figure."

"Exactly."

I knew he had a lot more to say after being cooped up on a plane for hours with no one but civilians around, but for a moment it seemed he'd talked himself out.

Then he asked, "Where you want to meet?"

This was going to be the hard part. "Well," I said, "actually, I was thinking we shouldn't meet. In case he's watching. I think it'd be better off if you trail me from a distance, watch my back, see if you can draw a bead on him."

I waited and listened. It sounded like baggage carousel information in the background.

"I can set you up in one of our safe apartments, call you a critical support agent for the paperwork, and leave it at that," I said. "I'll get you the address."

"Yeah. Makes sense." He said this, but in his voice I heard disappointment, a letdown that I wasn't going to meet him. He'd been excited to come here to work with me. I wondered if I wasn't actually stringing him along, fucking with whatever emotions he had. I wondered if I even felt anything.

"Shit. I want to see you, too, Oscar. You've got to believe that. It means a lot to me that you came right down. But I don't want him to know that I'm not working alone. I don't—"

"There's got to be some way we can meet."

I'd wrapped the phone cord around my finger so tight its tip was turning purple. I looked at the scar along my palm. I wasn't wearing a bandage anymore, but the plastic surgery was still in my future.

"We can meet," I said. "I'll text you the address of the safe apartment and head there to see you."

"Yeah," he said. "That sounds good." I heard relief in his voice.

"Okay. Call me back if you have questions."

We hung up. I looked at my computer screen and at the pictures of Ivan on my wall. He was out there. And now I had to find a way to lose him.

CHAPTER 43

The safe house I sent Linstrom to was downtown above the Embarcadero Center. No one but tourists ever wanted to be down in that area beyond work hours, so it made a perfect place for us to put up anyone coming in from out of town. Even if we were trying to protect and hide somebody local, it made a great location because they could blend in more easily among the tourists.

Maybe Linstrom would like it, and maybe he wouldn't. One thing for sure was that, after Anchorage, it was going to make him feel that he'd arrived in a place both very big and very urban. No green space down there, just concrete, water, and tall buildings—buildings probably twice as tall as the highest ones in Anchorage. With the Bay Bridge towering over the whole view it would make for more of a man-made wonder than Linstrom would ever see in the Great Land. He'd have an eyeful, for sure.

Now I just had to get to him—without being followed.

I thought of the familiar method of taking public transportation, jumping on and off cars like in the movies, and it actually sounded as if it might be worth a try.

I thought of Officer Cope in his favorite café, no harm having come to him, and the possibility that my own paranoia was taking over. But I didn't have time to play it any other way. If I wanted this case, wanted to go up against Ivan on my own—especially here in my own city where *he* was the fish out of water—I needed to play by my rules, take all precautions, and follow any hunch. Not second-guess myself. Not ever, not at all.

I'd need to plow straight ahead. With caution, but still.

The scar on my palm itched. I rubbed it gently against my thigh. This wasn't just a case anymore. Not since Trent, or even before that with Jason Andrews and my cut. No, this guy was following me across the country now, out of Alaska and to the city I called home. He wanted *me* now, and that left only one possible outcome. I had to find him and finish this, end it all on my own.

I grabbed my bag off the side chair of my cubicle and headed out for BART. It was just a couple of blocks to Civic Center station, through City Hall Plaza and its roaming droves of homeless. At night this was like the walk of the living dead. Ivan could be any of them, disguised in dirt, easily hidden out of my sight.

I cradled the grip of my weapon as I walked, certain I couldn't be too careful. Hiding in San Francisco wouldn't take much. Following someone, on the other hand, especially someone on the move, especially when you didn't know the city well, that was another story.

Entering the station, I took the escalator past the upper level for Muni passengers and all the way down to BART. With one of the new Clipper cards, I didn't have to worry about fare charges, overages or underages, or anything of the sort. With my iPhone I accessed a list of upcoming departure and arrival times. On the escalator down, I pulled up a random location in Berkeley, a restaurant I'd gone to once, and punched up transit directions. There was a train leaving in four minutes that would take me across the bay, and there I could transfer to another train to get to downtown Berkeley. That, or I could hop directions and come back across the bay to San Francisco. If I played it right, it would work.

On the platform, late Friday commuters and people going home after dinner in town waited patiently for their trains in neat rows. Black-marked areas on the floor designated where the car doors would open. People actually waited in order here, queued up for the next train or the one after that. Civic order and civility. They didn't stand too close to one another, but just close enough.

I waited at the bottom of the escalator, watching to see who came down after me. There was no stream of bodies at this hour, no sign of Ivan. Perhaps he had money to hire someone or had gotten an accomplice, or perhaps he was riding down to the platform on an escalator from another entrance. I couldn't be sure, but nor could I be too safe.

I told myself to calm down. *Vigilance.* The word popped into my head, followed by *paranoia.* I was in a world between the two, with no way to know where the line was or which side of it I was on.

The train headed for Dublin and Pleasanton came, and I got on. I watched the doors down the length of the track, checking to see even the last people who got on. Everyone looked more or less normal—couples or commuters or people from the Bay Area. Just folks getting onto a train. I checked the other passengers in my car. They looked okay. I felt just a little bit safe. But I had three more stops until West Oakland.

For some reason, Ivan only showed up in the summer every five years. Now he could disappear at any moment; he might disappear for months or even years at a time. If he had left that pattern and the white nights by coming to San Francisco, I couldn't know what schedule he'd take from here. I didn't want to go through this fear for the rest of my life. Whatever it took, I wanted him now.

I was up to this. That's what I was ready to say to Linstrom. I had passed all the agent tests—sparring training, criminology, and profiling—with flying colors. I'd even caused some damage to old Ivan, the fucker. I would get my Russian.

CHAPTER 44

Through the rest of the downtown stops—Powell, Montgomery, and Embarcadero—I watched who got on and who got off the train. From Embarcadero, we made our way under the water for the longest stretch between stops. The train rattled and shook as we picked up speed. If Ivan were on with me, all he'd need to do was pull the emergency brake and the entire load of passengers would be thrust into a world of uncertainty and darkness. Caught underneath all that water, we'd have to get out and walk to the nearest station. I'd be easy prey.

The lights flickered off and then on again. Off and on. We rattled through the darkness as passengers read their books, carried on their conversations, acted like nothing unusual was happening. I watched their slightest movements, waited for us to come back out.

Then, before I knew it, we'd popped back outside again and onto the elevated tracks through West Oakland. Elevated and clear and long, it was the stop I was waiting for and the vantage point I needed. I took a deep breath.

I pulled up the map feature on my phone and entered a location back downtown, near the safe apartment and searched for directions. Sure enough, the next train back under the bay would arrive at West Oakland in just under three minutes. Exactly as I wanted.

As the train slowed, I got ready by the door. When it stopped, I waited and watched passengers get off and a few lone men get on. The red lights flashed and the doors began closing. I stepped out. I reached the platform just as the doors closed. A lone conductor craned his head out the window and gave me a look like I was crazy. The doors slid back open all up and down the train.

"Watch the closing doors," the conductor said. "Next stop Lake Merritt. Lake Merritt is next." I stood watching, waiting to see if anyone would step out. If Ivan was here and he wanted to follow me, the only way he could would be to show himself now.

All up and down the train, the doors were open. No one moved. The doors closed. The train started to pull away.

I ran for the stairs, hearing the train barreling along, clacking down the tracks and not stopping—just as I had hoped. I ran down into the station and crossed to the other platform, got up to it just as the next train bound back for the city was pulling in. This one was far less crowded. I got right on, sat down, and waited for the doors. It'd be at least four minutes until my first train got to Lake Merritt, more until another was able to come back in the direction of West Oakland, even longer before it got back into San Francisco.

The doors closed, and the train started away. If I was being followed before, I didn't think I was now. I felt relief. If anyone had been out there, watching my movements, now I was alone.

I passed back under the bay, into San Francisco, and got off at Embarcadero. There I left the train car, walked up to street level, and headed straight for the safe apartment.

CHAPTER 45

My heart beat less quickly now; any sense of paranoia had left me feeling exhilarated and cool. Sweat dried on my forehead in the chill night air. I walked the streets with my head high and my eyes wide open.

At the safe-house building, I let myself in using a code to open the front door. At the apartment, the key was in the designated spot at the end of the hall. As it turned out, I was there before Linstrom. I freshened up and sat in the heavy desk chair to wait.

The apartment was barely a studio, nicely furnished but without a significant kitchen. Nationwide cutbacks made it just possible to fund this place on the department budget, but for now we kept it. It still came in handy more often than you might guess.

I closed my eyes and tried to calm my nerves. Pretty soon there was a knock, and when I opened the door, Linstrom wheeled his medium-size agent's suitcase over to the dresser and sat down heavily on the bed.

"I feel like I just walked all the way from Anchorage," he said. "And now I'm ready to eat a moose." He tilted his head. "You guys have moose burgers here, right?"

I smiled. "Of course we do. All sustainably farmed and fed with locally grown organic acorns, free of hormones, steroids, and antibiotics. Just the way you like it!"

He fell back onto the bed. When he sat up, he said, "Seriously, what can we get to eat?"

"We can order anything in. Whatever you want."

He tilted his head. "That bad, really?"

I leaned in and patted him on his knee. "That and I want you all to myself."

He looked surprised for a moment. I sat back fast and kept my hands in my lap. I started talking fast. "Why else do you think I called and asked you down here? I had to take two trains and make a crazy transfer just so I could meet you, all to make sure I wasn't being followed." I told him about Stephanie Harvey's murder, the crime scene, and the writing in blood. He knew the watchwords for terrorism, and it didn't escape either of us that Ivan knew them, too.

"He's got to be military," Linstrom said when I finally ran out of breath. He didn't point out my embarrassment, scoring some points in the process.

"I know. He joined the navy in 2001 and then went AWOL about six months later."

"What then?"

"Dead end."

He shook his head. "What about here?"

"We've got the same MO, an unknown blunt object as a murder weapon, and the knife cut on her side. I think he wants to say he didn't kill Adina Howard in Homer and dump her body in the Fishing Hole."

He nodded.

I noticed that he'd leaned forward, close enough to where he could put his hand on my knee. "You read the file?"

He bit down on his lips. "Mmm-hmm."

"So what, then? He saw what Vitali was doing and got him out of the way?"

"Then he decided to focus his full attention on you."

Linstrom had been doing his homework, keeping up with the case. "And nothing in Alaska since I left."

"He knew you got sent back here; maybe he's been watching you for a while."

"I have to be careful. I know."

This was where Linstrom really looked at me hard, as I knew he would. He was the one I wanted to be doing it, too, the only one I wanted to have this conversation with. Whether it meant anything about having feelings for him, I wasn't sure.

That was when he made his move: he reached out to touch my knee. I let him. Truth was, it felt good.

"What do you want to do?"

I got excited and stood up. "What do you think? I want to get this fucker. I want to bring him in on a hook!"

He pulled his hand in like it'd been burned. After a few moments, he said, "If these leads are real, you're closer than you've ever been. You're getting to him."

"And he's getting closer to me."

"That's the problem, Jess. That's why I'm worried."

There it was.

I shook my head. My voice went up in volume. "I want him. Running from Alaska is one thing, but running from where I live is another. This ends here and now." If I had had something to pound my hand on, I would have done it.

He nodded. "Okay. But I can't do this on an empty stomach."

I laughed. And then I smiled, and we were all right together. I didn't have to worry about where we were headed or what was going to be the status of *us* from now on. It was back to just being two agents, doing a job, working together, and eating to keep going. I sat down in the chair again.

I wanted Chinese; he wanted pizza.

We settled on Thai.

CHAPTER 46

That was how we ended up sleeping together. Call it a moment of weakness or me taking my eyes off the ball. It doesn't matter. But it happened. From there all I could do was hope I hadn't made a mistake.

After we finished, he lay next to me breathing loud enough that I could hear. Neither of us had moved in a while, and I wanted him to be asleep. I shifted, scooting toward the bathroom.

"What's up?" he asked.

"Bathroom."

I went in and stood in front of the mirror. Looking back at me was a good-looking woman, a woman who deserved to get laid once in a while—and not in a bad way either. I deserved to get my swerve on, my jollies, my boat floated. This was something I could use regularly. Forget feelings, sentimentality, vulnerability; if Linstrom had to have those things, I'd worry about it later. For now, I just wanted to get off.

I barked out a laugh, surprising myself. It sounded so odd that I laughed again. Linstrom would think I was going crazy. He could. I washed my face and ran a washcloth over my sex. Then I threw it in the trash. The Bureau could buy a new one.

When I came out, I was as naked as when I'd gone in. Linstrom lay on his side, the sheet over his waist and legs, his chest looking good.

"Glad to know they have gyms up there in the bush."

"I work out," he said, "but mostly I just lift animals. Animals and guns. You know how it is."

"I do. Cross-country skiing like a *motherfucker.*"

Skiing was all I'd done in my Alaska winter. When the sun set at three in the afternoon, and the trails were the only places lit up, you didn't have much choice.

"What are you doing?" I asked.

"Why?"

"What's that look on your face?"

"Oh," he said. "I'm just admiring the view."

I looked down, checking myself and seeing the same me I saw in the mirror every morning. The same naked body that no man had seen in a while.

He opened the sheet, lifting it off of him and inviting me underneath. "Please," he said. "Be my guest."

CHAPTER 47

The next morning, over an ordered-in breakfast, I told him how it would go.

"You're not going to like this."

He put down his egg sandwich and just stared at me. "Not a good way to start, Harding."

"I don't care. I've got to get this out. This is going to be the last time I see you in a while."

"What? I just came—"

I held up a hand, trying to head him off. "Listen. Just listen to me for a minute."

He nodded, sat still. "But we just—" Then he took a deep breath and waited. "Okay. I'm listening."

"I want you to shadow me, follow me everywhere I go. You see me, but I don't let on that I see you. If we're lucky, maybe you see him. That's what I'm hoping. If nothing else, I want you to be there when he makes a move."

"I have a week, Harding. Ten days max." He knit his eyebrows. This wasn't going over well. "And you know he'll move *how*? What if he doesn't even follow you?"

"I know he will. He's going to do *some*thing. When I follow this Harvey case, he's going to trip. There's a reason he wants me on it, and I feel like there's something he wants to say. This sick fuck, he thinks there's a connection between us."

"Maybe there is." Linstrom pointed his chin at my hand, so I shoved it under my leg.

"I'm getting that taken care of. I've seen a doctor already."

"It's not—" He smiled. "I'm sorry, Harding, but it's not the hand. How would you look at this if you were on the outside, watching another agent? If you were watching me?"

"I know." I looked down at my eggs and hash browns and suddenly I didn't want anything else to eat. And I didn't want to talk. I didn't strictly know what I was doing. So I stood up, scooped my things off the bed, and whisked them into the bathroom to get dressed.

I put on my socks first. Why my socks? I didn't know. But then my pants, my bra, and finally my shirt. I left my panties on a hook on the back of the bathroom door for Linstrom to ponder.

When I came out, he was standing, pacing in a towel.

I said, "That's the way it's got to be. You're either with me or you're not, and you're the only one I want on my side."

"I know. I know." He held up his hands and then let them drop. "Give me an address where we start."

I gave him my apartment address, told him that I'd be leaving at noon to head to Stephanie Harvey's and that, from there, I'd do what I could with my leads. He said it was all right with him.

"So you're not going to let on you see me?" he asked.

"*If* I see you, then no. And *he* better *not* see you."

"I know. I saw what happened to the last guy you took home."

It felt like Lindstrom had just punched me in the gut. I ached for all the girls Ivan had gotten to and felt even worse about Trent because that had been my fault.

"Thanks for that," I said and walked out. I left Linstrom to finish eating, get himself dressed, and find a good map of the city on his own.

CHAPTER 48

My own apartment was less than ten blocks from Stephanie Harvey's. She lived at Valencia and Twenty-Fifth Street, and I was down on Twentieth, on the very east side of the Mission, almost over to Potrero Hill. I lived in one of the new redevelopments that were popping up in the neighborhood. My own place had floor-to-ceiling windows overlooking the street and was a two-level loft with the bedroom upstairs—another way to fight my fear of heights, perhaps. It would be a nice place to have Linstrom stay for a little while, when and if I was safe.

Big windows—I've always loved that idea, and when I saved enough to buy something, that was the first item on my list. Truth be told, the Bureau doesn't pay all that badly. With the overtime, · meals you eat while you're working, expenses to follow every lead on a case, eventually you wind up with a little savings. Sure, I work close to eighty hours a week, but the fact is I hardly even notice. Hip-deep in chasing a scumbag, it's hard to keep perspective on the other things that are supposed to make up a "normal life." It's all the job, and who cares about the rest.

On the other hand, a good lay every now and then or even a reasonable relationship can do wonders for the disposition. I caught myself whistling coming out of the shower, and then again when I was drying my hair. I had to give myself a stern, get-serious make-over with eye shadow and mascara so I'd appear to be the same agent I was the day before if Ivan was watching.

If I was lucky, he didn't know where I lived, or maybe that was too much to hope for. I wanted him to see me when I went near Stephanie Harvey's, not before.

To walk would have been easy, but instead I took a cab. Better for Ivan not to think I lived too close. I phoned for a taxi and waited by my windows, drinking coffee until it showed up.

I sent the cabbie down to Chavez, then over to Valencia and back up to Twenty-Fifth. More of the familiar paranoia or a slight move to make things cloudier, I didn't know. And I didn't question.

It was a rare sunny Saturday in August, and the hipsters were out walking their dogs, drinking coffee, and waiting in line for brunch throughout the Mission. Some would tell you August is the foggiest, coldest time of year in San Francisco—even Mark Twain is reported to have said it, famously, even though he never did. The truth is the Mission gets its share of sunny days. Come see for yourself.

On Cesar Chavez, the day laborers were out waiting, hoping to get picked up to make a few dollars on a Saturday. On Valencia, though, white twenty-somethings lived in a wholly different world. With tight jeans, torn T-shirts, and horn-rimmed glasses, they lived to define irony, making coolness into nerdiness and nerdiness cool. I'd seen enough of the eighties to know that I definitely didn't need to go back again for more, so I never understood the appeal. Especially the mustaches: I had no idea what they thought was good about those. Then again, they weren't asking.

In Stephanie Harvey's apartment, her body was gone. She'd been bagged and tagged, and a rush autopsy was scheduled for later in the afternoon. Even on a Saturday, anything could get done in the name of counterterrorism.

The apartment was so clearly not that of a terrorist, however; and the words *dirty bomb* could have meant anything from the bowel movement someone left in her crapper to the way she did

her makeup, her sexual proclivity, or the actual concept of killing people with an explosive made from radioactive material. To
anyone looking at it objectively, the first three would seem a hell
of a lot more likely than the fourth. Still, here was the diligence of
Homeland Security, and I was on the job.

Linstrom had been right that Ivan had military experience,
that much I still had to look into. A minor mystery to solve in a
world of bigger ones I hoped would lead me to my perp: Ivan the
Terrible, Ivan the Killer, Ivan the Turd.

Ivan the Daylight Killer.

In San Francisco, he'd left his white nights and full northern
exposure for a new set of particulars. What would he do now?
Kill only during the day? Or did he not care about his summer
white nights pattern anymore? Time of death for Stephanie Harvey
showed late Thursday night, so perhaps he'd let that slide in favor
of coming after me. It wasn't an idea I relished.

I poked around the apartment for the next hour and a half.
Partly this was for show, to spend time there and let my tails find
me, and partly to see what I could find. I knew I wasn't going to
break the case open and hoped I wouldn't find anything else left
especially for me.

I went over the bathroom, the kitchen, and the living room, all
more carefully than I normally would have. Other than the history
of a struggle in the living room, close enough to what I'd found in
Samantha Parker's, there wasn't much to see. I didn't find anything.

When I'd spent enough time in the apartment, I walked outside
and up Valencia. I let a few taxis pass, watching for anyone hanging
around, someone following me: Linstrom or Ivan, I wanted to see
if I noticed any signs.

After a while, I cabbed it back to the office and went up to
my floor, which was mostly deserted on a Saturday. In my cubicle,
the files had shown up from Homer, my query of anyone with the

last name of Nikolaevsk. There wasn't much to go through, just a few guys with thick beards who didn't look like anybody I knew. Then, there he was: buried halfway through the pile was a series of intake forms and fingerprints of my man Ivan, calling himself Vitali Nikolaevsk. The pictures looked just like Ivan Homer's driver's license taped to my wall. All the charges were like Cope had told me: public drunkenness, fighting, assault, disturbing the peace. Then they ended abruptly in the middle of August 2001.

Nothing more added from there.

I fired up my computer, ready to try for more on my man's military service. Maybe that would give some key to his five-year absences. For our own armed forces' tours of duty, it didn't make sense; five years was too long for someone to go overseas and not have time off.

So he'd gone AWOL and never come back.

As a Russian Old Believer, he wasn't likely to want to protect and serve the United States. That made sense. But on the other hand, he wasn't likely to want to defend Mother Russia either. The Old Believers had been persecuted there since the sixteen hundreds, when they broke from the Orthodox church. They'd fled Russia close to fifty years ago, so he wasn't likely to feel a heavy kinship with the motherland.

Then again, he'd been thrown out of Nikolaevsk, ostracized by the Old Believers, and spoke fluent Russian. So maybe Russia was a place he would go.

All this went through my mind as the computer got itself started up. I needed an upgrade.

I scanned online to refresh my knowledge of the contemporary Russian military. Post-USSR, our files designated the armed forces of the Russian Federation at a three on our international military scale. With us as the only consistent one on the scale, and the smallest countries at a five, this put Russia right in the middle.

With just over a million troops, they were not the first country we'd call in a skirmish, but they were in the top half of our list. In 2007, their tour of duty had been cut to one year, so that didn't fit Ivan's five-year schedule either. Perhaps I was going about it wrong.

Fishing was another possibility, a job that would take him away and bring him back every now and then—more often than every five years, but who was to say Ivan didn't play by his own rules. Maybe he had a larger pattern that went beyond Alaska.

I started a new search for crimes that resembled what I'd seen in Alaska, the case specifics he'd established there. It was when I took the search international, started scanning Interpol, that interesting connections popped up.

Using Interpol wasn't part of our standard operating procedure, but it should have been. I tried to remember to check it as often as I could, but that didn't happen enough, especially when I was spending my time running down murder after murder in Alaska, in and out of the woods. Now I knew I'd been wrong not to make more time for it. I knew immediately, as soon as the other Daylight cases started popping up.

The first I saw was Greenland in 2003; then Iceland and Norway in 2005, followed by Russia in 2007. All of the victims were young women, bound, tied with barbed wire, cut in various ways, hit on the head with something, plenty of blood at the scene. All in places north of the sixtieth parallel—places that had close to nineteen hours of sunlight every day in summer.

This was the pattern I'd grown familiar with.

Some had writing in blood at the scene, some didn't. I wasn't sure what that was about, but guessed at a language barrier. The pattern made for every two years, in the summer, in white nights.

What was it with this guy and the sun?

CHAPTER 49

It started with Greenland in 2003: three women, all in their twenties, last seen after ten p.m., killed in their own apartments in a bloody, brutal style. No writing.

Then Iceland: three women in 2005 all abducted from locations close to their homes, no witnesses, daylight conditions out on the nights they disappeared. Similar carnage at their apartments, hands tied with wire, some writing in blood left behind at the scene.

Same year in Norway: one woman, similar conditions, *a lot* of writing in blood.

Then came the murders I knew of: Alaska 2006, seven brutal murders of women in their twenties, all in the general vicinity of Anchorage, ranging down to Juneau and as far north as Fairfax. All committed in the height of white nights. Women left in bloody apartments, with writing everywhere, blood on the walls, and almost a total lack of leads. Fortunately, from the Interpol perspective, none of the internal failings of our investigation were evident. None of the infighting, disagreements, lost opportunities, and mistakes showed up through this lens.

I started reading through the files from Russia and stopped. I felt strange.

I stood up and looked over the tops of the other cubicles. I didn't see anyone around. Not a big surprise for a Saturday afternoon, but I could hear keyboards clicking away in the office. People were on the floor. No one was watching me, and yet my nerves were on full alarm.

I sat down hard on my chair and let out a deep sigh. All around me on the walls of my cube were pieces of evidence from my career: postings, perps I'd caught up with, cases I'd solved. In some ways, it looked like a wall of accomplishments—or trophies, even. Then I saw Ivan: Smitty's sketch and the driver's license photo among the others. All of these tacked up like things I had done. But how good was I? Here my main perp had committed similar crimes in at least four more countries, one if not more after I started my investigation. So many more possible threads, so many more crime scenes and leads and women's bodies. So many undeterred deaths.

So many possibilities that I had no idea what the hell I was doing.

I rested my head in my hands for a few breaths, thinking it all through.

Then I started swearing softly, loud enough to get it out but quiet enough that no one else would hear. Sure, you learned as you went along, got better every year on the job, ideally. But had I really missed all of these for this long?

It wasn't a realization I was ready to face.

Suddenly the whole plan felt like it was unraveling in front of me: Linstrom following me around, me ignoring him, even the idea that we'd had sex and that he wasn't going to make a big deal out of it, or want to shack up and do it again.

"Fuck." I said it out loud and felt just a little bit better.

I got up, pushed my chair in, and walked to the bathroom. There, I stooped over the sink. I wiped my eyes and looked at myself in the mirror: all smeared mascara and eyeliner. I looked a mess. Suddenly I retched. Nothing but bile came up. I coughed it out and washed it down the drain, tried to rinse the taste out of my mouth with handfuls of water.

What if everything I thought about him coming here was wrong? What if I'd called down Oscar for nothing?

"Jesus."

I looked up and saw my own face in the mirror, my eyes bleary from tearing up. There I was, along with Marlene Roberts standing right behind me.

"You look like shit, Harding. What the fuck?"

I didn't turn around; instead I just hung my head over the sink and spit. When I could speak, I said, "Thought I'd never see *you* here on a Saturday."

"Overtime. Got to pay down these credit cards. What's going on with you?"

"Just my time of the month. You know."

She chuckled. "Don't bullshit me, Harding. Something is up."

I met her eyes, realized how serious she was. "A rough day, you know?" I stood and took a few paper towels, wiped at the corners of my eyes.

Roberts started washing her hands at the sink next to me. "Sure, I know those days. But you're not supposed to, Harding. Come on, you're the Golden Girl."

"Not today." I shook my head. "I think I just crashed to the ground. I don't know which way is up."

"No offense," she said, "but it's okay. You just might make the rest of us look better." She reached past me and took some paper towels, dried her hands. Then she patted me on the shoulder. "Come on, you know you work your tail off to make yourself one of the best agents on the floor. Give it a break for one day. Just be a person."

Our eyes met in the mirror, and I could see she meant well.

I nodded. "Okay. I hear you."

"We're all just human here." She handed me some paper towels to dry my face. "What's going on?"

"I—" I didn't say anything else, just leaned over and held both sides of the sink. Then I said, "I think there's a madman out there who's trying to kill me."

Once I'd gotten the words out, I let my shoulders slump. My legs went weak for a moment, and I made it through a few hard breaths. Then I felt about 111 percent better, as if I'd let a weight off my shoulders.

"Is this true?" She had been asking me questions, ones I hadn't even heard.

I nodded. "Come back to my cubicle with me. I need to sit down."

CHAPTER 50

In front of my computer, I showed Roberts the pictures of Ivan from 2001 and from now, as well as the case files and the pictures of what he'd done to the women in Alaska. I showed her what he did to Trent in Anchorage right in front of me, and she pulled my hand away from my mouse to look at the palm.

"The guy who did this to you—he's here?" She pointed at the scar with her finger.

"Not exactly," I said, and told her about Jason Andrews, the chase, and Ivan helping me down from the side of the truck.

"Shit." She had sworn more than a few times as I told the story. That was before I really got into what had gone on in Alaska in 2006, all the red tape and male bullshit I'd had to fight through. When I got into that part of it, she started saying "Fuck."

"So this is why I want to take care of it myself."

Roberts was my friend, but I'd never opened up to her about a case like this. I'd never opened up like this to *anyone* in San Francisco.

She got up and hugged me.

"Jesus," she said into my ear. "What are we going to do?"

"I'm telling you. I don't know. That's how I'm fucking up."

"How sure are you about all this?" She looked at me for a few moments.

I nodded. What else could I say?

"Have you been sleeping?"

I laughed. "Maybe too well."

"You need to eat. I always approach a case more clearly after a meal."

I realized I was hungry, I had to admit.

"Look," she said, "how about we get out of here for an hour? A little air helps the thinking. Let me watch your back for a bit."

"I could eat."

She shoved my bag into my hand and pulled me out of my cubicle toward the elevators. "Come on. Real people take breaks, Harding."

We went downstairs and across the street, to one of the nicer restaurants in the area. She ordered a beer and convinced me to have one, too, for my "nerves."

"In my family, if something's wrong we feed people," she said. "That's what we do."

She ordered fish tacos and french fries. I got the tacos, but substituted a salad for the fries.

I listened to her talk, all the time distracted by thoughts of Ivan, where he might be.

Then she started opening up about herself. She was from Oakland, the first in her family to graduate college and, as far as she knew, the first one from her block to work a drug case from the justice side of the law.

I thought about telling her where I grew up in Massachusetts, and how my father had unraveled into alcoholism until he was nothing more than a drunk; how my mother tried to run and never managed to get far enough away. I didn't say any of it.

I had joined the Bureau. That was my story. I worked my hardest to get away from Pittsfield to where I wanted to land. I busted my ass and never looked back.

We both ate things we shouldn't have, drank beer. Then I told her about Linstrom, that we'd slept together, but not that he was an agent.

"Shit, girl? Are you crazy? That's great!"

"Probably. I could be crazy."

Roberts craned her neck, looking every which way out the window she could. "You really think a serial killer is out there right now watching?"

Something about the way she said it made me doubt myself. I turned to look, too, saw just a narrow downtown street and a flood of cars.

I said, "I don't know."

She shook her head. "Sometimes we never do. But listen, I'm glad you found yourself a man. That's a good thing...Where is he now? Your boyfriend. I want to meet him."

"Not today."

She handed me my purse. "Call this man!"

I looked at her—here she was, telling me what to do. In less than a single day, I'd had sex with Linstrom and now Roberts was telling me what to do. I was losing control, becoming "a normal."

"Tell the man you're thinking about him."

"But—" The thing was, it was true. "Shit," I said. "You're probably right." I fished my phone out and called him. He answered right away.

"How's that lunch?" he asked. "Looks like you two are having a fine old time in there. Me? I'm out on the street!"

I turned and glanced out the window but couldn't see him. "Where are you?"

"Trade secret. I'd like to tell you, but—"

"Then you'd have to kill me. I know, I know."

"Exactly. But those tacos look good. Got some for old Oscar?"

Roberts sipped her beer, checking something on her BlackBerry and typing with her thumbs.

I turned away from her and whispered into my phone, "Have you seen anyone? Anything out there?"

"No. I got you at Harvey's apartment, when you went in. Nothing and nobody and then the same when you left. Nobody hopping a cab to keep up. Nada."

"Tell me this," I said, "do you think I'm crazy?"

"Of course I do. That's why you're so wonderful."

I let him wait that one out. He was starting to sound more like a lovestruck boyfriend than an agent I could count on.

"No," he said, "I trust your instincts. You're one of the best agents I've worked with. We're doing this, and we're going to keep doing it right."

Roberts made a face at me, started waving her hands that I should hurry up and tell him something sexy. That was when her phone started to ring. She shut it up and then in a few seconds it rang again.

Finally she looked at her phone and swore.

"I gotta go," I said to Linstrom.

Roberts typed in a text—a long one—and signaled the waiter for our bill. Then she put down cash on the table. "Wouldn't you know it?" She shook her head. "Here it is a Saturday afternoon in August, and my husband actually expects me to come home. Can you believe that? Doesn't want me at work all day. Such a crazy man."

I protested the money, but she wouldn't give up.

"Just deal with it," she said finally. "I'm buying your lunch. You can't deny me." She winked. "Let me walk you back across the street. We'll get you the proper protective detail."

"I'm okay," I said. "I'll get back to the office. You can trust me."

She cocked her head at that, as though I was some rare creature that needed study. "You sure?"

I pointed to our building. We could see it through the window. "Yes," I said. "*Trust me.*"

"Fucking Harding." She pinched my cheek and then leaned in to hug me tight. "You're still too good for the rest of us, but you're starting to come around."

I didn't know what this meant about where I should take the Daylight Killer case, but she seemed all right in the world in a way

I wasn't, in a way I wanted to be. I didn't know what separated us, couldn't even begin to understand.

Finally, she agreed to let me stay.

When she had left, I forced myself to sit back and finish my beer. I looked around: no one seemed to notice or care; the world kept right on spinning. That was when I heard a familiar voice in the back of my head.

I called Linstrom as fast as I could. "He's here."

Linstrom didn't have to ask who. "Where?"

"I'm not sure. But I can feel him. He's watching me right now."

"What? Where?"

"I know it." I sat up as straight as I could and scanned the room. All of a sudden, I felt sober as a hawk. I didn't doubt myself anymore. I *knew*.

It was time to move.

"How do you know?" He let the question hang in the air just long enough to find out I didn't care about the answer. "Not that it matters," he said, less than convincingly.

"It doesn't. We act, not analyze. You with me?"

I waited for my answer, knowing there was only one thing I wanted to hear.

"I'm with you. What's our play?"

"I'm going to walk outside and head south toward Market. Trail me. *Find him*."

"Just lead the way, Jess. I'm here."

It felt good to hear it. There was no doubt about that.

I knew I could trust myself, trust what I knew. Ivan was under my skin, and I was ready to use that against him.

CHAPTER 51

I went outside, looked around at the chilled, windblown street. The sun was out, shining, but it felt cold.

I was in the financial district on a Saturday afternoon, the streets filled more with tourists than anything else. We were close to Union Square shopping. People passed along the sidewalk in both directions.

Linstrom wanted to call in backup, but I told him to wait. "Once we know he's on my trail, *then* we make the call."

"But how long until we know?"

I shook my head. "Not long. I'll know." I held my hand up. "You see me?"

"I do."

I still hadn't seen Linstrom *or* Ivan. I hoped it meant Linstrom was good at this.

"Okay," I said into the phone, "here goes," and I hung up.

I walked south, listening to my inner voices, checking people's faces all around me. At every corner I stopped, looked all around, trying to see Ivan. He was never there.

People passed me on the street as if I wasn't anybody in particular. Just a girl in a suit like any other. No one seemed to notice me. I saw tourists buying T-shirts, men on their phones, women in too-high shoes.

When I hit Market, I felt as if something was wrong. Ivan was gone.

I pulled out my cell to dial Linstrom, cutting to my right across a plaza, heading for Bush.

Linstrom's phone rang in my ear. I had visions and ideas of him not answering, of it going straight to voice mail, and felt responsible already. All I could do if something happened would be to run the streets looking for him, hoping to see him before Ivan pulled him into an alley.

If the same thing happened to him that happened to Trent, I would never forgive myself.

And then he answered his cell and my whole world fell back into place. "Hey. No sign here."

"Where are you?"

I could hear the traffic on his end of the phone and somehow make it out as different from the traffic all around me. Different horns, I guess.

"I'm here."

"Where?"

"Close by. I see you. I'm about a block back. On Bush, near Battery. Where you headed?"

"I'm coming toward you. Something feels wrong."

"Okay. What do we do? Where you want to go?"

I stopped and tried to conjure my best mental image of downtown San Francisco. I was never any good at remembering all of the crisscrossing vertical, horizontal, and diagonal streets. None of them had names based on any order. Above me I saw a tall statue of several naked men operating a huge machine of some sort. Two of them looked like they were trying to have sex with its lever.

I told Linstrom to hang on and pulled up the map feature on my phone. While I waited for it to locate me, I said, "You still there?"

"Here, Harding."

"Okay. One second. What do you see?"

He laughed. "I see tall buildings, a gym that's called 24 Hour Fitness. Jesus, do they really have gyms open twenty-four hours here?"

"Yeah. Really." I looked at my phone again, realized that it wouldn't let me access the map while I was on a call. "Fuck."

I listened for him and heard nothing.

"Linstrom? Oscar?"

I checked my phone, saw only the map, no bar inviting me to return to my call. He was gone.

"Shit." I started to jog north and then west on Bush, toward Linstrom, touching the screen buttons to call him again. Something felt wrong.

I ran and listened to the rings. People moved to get out of my way if they saw me, and the ones who didn't I dodged around. I felt like the football player in some old airline commercial. Tall buildings floated above me and blotted out direct sun. Linstrom felt somehow very close and also very far. Each block looked long enough to take several full minutes to run. I had flats on, but they weren't the right shoes, not to run in. At this time on a Saturday, flagging a cab would get me nowhere but stuck in traffic. I jogged as best I could.

His phone continued to ring and then voice mail picked up.

"Hi, this is Oscar Linstrom, I can't take your call right now so—"

"Fuck. Oscar?"

Beep.

"Oscar? Oh, shit. Where are you?"

I saw just a long block up Bush and a slight hill, buildings all around me. The sidewalks weren't crowded, but the cars parked along the street made it hard to see far ahead or to scan the people on the other side.

"Oscar?" I waited a moment then gave up. "Call me."

I kept going, starting to breathe hard. Suddenly the beer and the tacos returned. I burped and tasted fried fish. Acid and bile rose up the back of my throat.

I pushed myself the last thirty feet to Sansome and looked around: up Bush and down toward Market. I couldn't see any signs of Oscar.

My phone rang and buzzed in my hand at the same time. The screen said, "Oscar Linstrom." I stopped running.

"Hey. Where are you?"

"*I am here, in your San Francisco.*"

That voice: both strange and too familiar. I swore to myself. It was him, *Ivan*, on Oscar's phone.

"What do you want? Tell me what it is, where he is, and I'll give it to you." I sounded desperate, and it made me sick. Looking around, I tried to see someone with a phone, someone who was Ivan talking to me and holding Linstrom at bay. Above me the buildings started to swirl and sway like trees in a breeze. I caught a street sign and then leaned hard against a newspaper dispenser. It wobbled, but held.

"Jessica? Jess Harding? Are you there?"

I stood fast, pulling myself up by the sign.

"Where are you?"

He sucked his teeth at me, scolding. "*Tsk tsk.* You know that I am here with your *Oscar*. Your friend, the agent Oscar Linstrom from Anchorage."

"Let me speak to him!" I raged at the phone. When I heard his laughter, I stopped and shut up.

"Oh, I will let you two speak, Agent Harding. Or can I call you Jess?" When I didn't answer, he said, "You will speak to him in its just and due time."

"Okay." Now I held onto the post with one hand, standing on two feet and taking deep breaths. The jogging had definitely not helped matters, but now I could catch my breath again, calm myself. After I started to feel less queasy, I asked, "What do you want me to do, Ivan?"

"You are where? Close by to us, are you?"

"Don't hurt him. Okay? You haven't hurt him, have you?" Visions of what happened to Trent flashed through my head. I saw Vitali Nikolaevsk in the woods, his own face peeled back from the skull. "I'll give you whatever you want."

He laughed a little, two short exhales, and I saw red. I wanted to get my hands on him and kill him with my fingers. The scar on my palm burned. I transferred the phone into my left hand and pulled my gun from the small of my back. I slipped my finger around the trigger.

"Let me see you, Ivan. Just come see me, and I'll do whatever you want. You can have me for your sick fucking games."

"You will do this, will you? And you know what it is that I want?"

I started walking again, heading south toward Market. Linstrom and Ivan had to be south or west of me, and I took my shot at a guess.

"You want *me*," I said. "What else would you come to San Francisco for? For some reason you want me, and I'm going to give you all you'd ever imagine."

Again with the short laughs. "Do not try to sound tough."

"Does that make you horny, Ivan? Do you want me?"

"No!" Now he was angry. "You do not talk like that. Do not, Harding. I—"

"Why not, Ivan? You kill all these girls, so many over the years, and you want to fuck them, don't you? But they won't fuck you, will they?" I kept walking. I could hear my own blood pumping in my ears. Ivan stayed quiet. "Isn't that what makes you so angry, Ivan? That these girls won't let you fuck them, or that you can't get it up? That's why you have to hurt them, isn't it?"

Now his voice was small and hard through the connection. "Do not," he said.

I started feeling less queasy; the buildings weren't looming over me from above. I could see the street ahead, and it kept level. "Why not, Ivan? Does it hurt your feelings that I know this? Is this what they said to you in Nikolaevsk? Is this why Nina kicked you out?"

"Stop it."

"I know you, Ivan. Isn't that what you like about me? That I know you and you think you know me?"

I got to the three-way corner of Sutter and Sansome and Market. I saw kiosks and street signs and a Muni trolley. The Citigroup Center stood officious in its Greek style with Ionic pillars.

"Can you see me, Ivan? Do you know where I am?"

I waited, turning to look up Sutter and crossing the street toward Market. On the wide sidewalk, I tried to see them but couldn't. A man in a gray suit noticed me and then jumped back, horrified. I realized I had my gun in my hand, blatantly holding it out by my side. "Federal agent," I told him. "And mind your own fucking business."

He turned away, kept on walking.

"I'm here, Ivan," I said into the phone. "Can you see me? Do you want to make a trade?"

CHAPTER 52

Ivan's voice came through the phone heavy and harsh; I'd riled him, gotten to him exactly as I'd hoped.

"Yes, I can see you now, *Jess*. Come slowly up Sutter Street and then you see us. We are here."

I started up Sutter, walking slowly, my gun down by my side. With the drinks and the running, I could not have hit a person at thirty feet with any accuracy just a few minutes before, but now I was breathing what felt like clean, fresh air. My blood had stopped pumping in my ears. The buildings had returned to their complete resting state.

"Just let me see you, Ivan," I said. One shot was all I wanted; one shot at a perp was all I'd practiced to get. I'd shot for hours and hours at the range over the years, countless targets, hoping I would never need to fire a round in the line of duty. Now I felt the opposite; I just wanted my *one shot*. One chance. I wanted Ivan dead by my own hand.

"Ivan?" I asked. "Where *are* you?"

"Listen to your boyfriend, Jess. Because you are so confident and talk to me like this. Now listen."

The voice on the phone changed to Oscar's. "*Jess, I—*" He coughed, a sound that was both wet and painful, and that was all. I had a vision of what Ivan did to Trent.

"Yes. You like this? This how your boyfriend sound like with my knife in his side. He squeals a little bit when he ask for you."

"No!" I started to run. "Don't fucking hurt him, Ivan."

"You hear this? Like a little balloon losing its air."

"Don't do this, Ivan."

"He sound like a girl that I cut, Harding. Just like the girls."

I started running faster, pounding my flats against the sidewalk and waving my gun. In a minute, I was at the next corner, with a Citibank to my right and a darker Union Bank on my left. In front of me, Montgomery ran one way in the direction of Market.

Behind me I heard a woman scream.

"Turn around."

I did as I was told, and there was Ivan, holding Linstrom in front of him, a hunting knife pressed to Linstrom's throat. It was the same big knife he had shown me in Anchorage. Linstrom looked worse than just hurt, like he was also drugged. He slumped against Ivan's body.

They had stepped out of a building, some door or doorway I'd run right past, not guessing it might be unlocked.

Then I saw Ivan's other hand pressing the hilt of another knife to Linstrom's side.

"No," I said under my breath.

I pocketed my phone and brought both hands to my gun, holding it at shoulder height, trained on them. Ivan shook his head. From that distance, maybe twenty-five feet, it was a hard shot—with Oscar blocking most of Ivan. Hard, but not impossible.

"This is not good idea," Ivan said. I could hear him now without our phones; his voice sounded scratchy from that distance. It sounded just like the one I'd heard in my head when I got to Samantha Parker's.

Someone across the street yelled "Police!" and another woman screamed.

"Federal agent," I called back. "Clear this street! There's nothing to see here so stay the fuck out of my line of fire!"

Some people scattered; others stood watching. From the corner of my eye, I saw a kid of about twenty standing in the street, holding his phone up to video us or take pictures.

"Go, kid! Leave!" I yelled, taking another step toward Ivan and Oscar. "Everyone get away from here!"

I brought all of my attention to Ivan. "Tell me what you want. Whatever you need, we can make this happen."

He waved his knife in the light, the bigger one, and somehow even in these light-blocking caverns of tall buildings, the polished metal caught a ray of sun. He lucked into a direct beam of light, striking me in the eyes and blinding me for a moment. I ducked to my right, moving away. He still waved the knife, its blade shimmering.

"This light," he said. "So beautiful here, don't you think so? So strong."

"Why do you do it, Ivan? Why do you kill them?"

He nodded and stepped toward the building, putting Linstrom farther between us.

"This fifth time I have seen you like this, Harding. You not even know them all. You don't know."

I kept the gun up. "You want it to end like this, Ivan? Here so far from your white nights? From Nikolaevsk, your home? From Alaska?"

He sucked his teeth. "This is not the end, Jess. And Nikolaevsk, it does not matter." He shrugged dismissively. "Those people, they know nothing of me."

"Why the girls, Ivan?" I pressed him, stepping closer again, hoping to distract him into a stupid move. He brought the knife back to Oscar's throat.

"That is good distance," he said.

"Oscar? Can you hear me?"

Something dim passed through Linstrom's eyes, but I could tell he wasn't with it. Drugs, I hoped.

"He hears you."

I stood still, letting the moment pass. From not far off, I heard a police siren. If I was lucky, they would show up soon and close off the street. Ivan would be trapped at both ends, but behind him was the door into a building. I had no idea where it led. Or how he'd gotten me here. But he had. Both of us.

Oscar's shirttail was out of his pants, dripping blood down his leg.

"Let him go, Ivan."

He backed up another few steps toward the door. It was propped open with a brick; all he had to do was kick it out, then let the door close behind him, and it would lock. He would be gone.

A siren squawked from behind me. Out of the corner of my eye, I saw a police cruiser pull up fast at the corner of Montgomery and Sutter, its lights flashing. It rocked to a hard stop. Blues and reds played off the glass of the Citibank building. A bullhorn sounded from the cruiser's roof, and an officer's voice said, "Drop your weapons, both of you. This is the police."

Then two officers were out of the car, pointing their guns. On the far side of the car, the driver still held a mic. "Listen and comply," he said through the loudspeaker. "We do not want to shoot."

"Federal agent!" I tossed my wallet behind me, toward them. "This man is a serial killer and has apprehended my partner. I require assistance."

The closer cop picked up my wallet, still holding his gun in our direction, and checked it for a badge. He nodded to his partner, said, "She checks out."

The other officer spoke to me now without his megaphone. "What do you want us to do?"

I took a step closer to Ivan. He inched back.

"Get my partner to medical assistance," I told the cops. Then I made my move: I kept my feet still and leaned in to let my weight give me a bit of momentum before I started the short run from where I stood. Ivan twisted the knife in Oscar's gut at the same time, and Oscar screamed in a new, high-pitched way that sounded bad. But I didn't stop, and Ivan didn't slit Oscar's throat.

Instead he pushed Oscar toward me, kicked the brick away from the door and retreated into the building. I could see stairs inside. Oscar fell to my side, but I didn't catch him; instead I went for the door and lunged as it closed.

Ivan was pulling it shut, hard, and I knew I had only one chance. I thrust out my left hand, the good one, reaching for the door with my fingers, knowing they were the only things I could get in its way before it closed and locked behind him.

I was more ready to lose my fingers than I was Ivan. Even now this doesn't strike me as impossible. I winced in anticipation, knowing my fingers could get crushed in the slam or sliced off at the knuckle. At the time, it was the only thing I knew to try; I didn't have a chance to come up with anything else. With my gun hand, I reached for the door's handle but none was there.

The door slammed shut. I felt a searing pain in my hand.

And then, nothing.

CHAPTER 53

I pulled my left arm back from the door and it swung open to reveal an empty stairwell. My fingers hurt—hurt really fucking bad—but they weren't bleeding and I still had them. It was more than I had hoped for.

Before me stood a set of stairs that led only one direction: up. I didn't stop; I ran right to them, hoping I wasn't far behind Ivan.

The stairwell was standard: just plain white walls and green painted steps. I hit the first landing and saw more stairs. I looked up and in the middle of the stairwell could see a ray of light shining down from above—high above. I stopped short, and in the quiet I heard someone else running, making swift time up the stairs.

I kept on running after him, pulling at the railings with my left hand to get my body up as fast as I could. My fingers hurt but they worked, and that was good enough for now. I swung around each landing gun-first but didn't see Ivan. He hadn't stopped and didn't plan to.

I tried a few of the doors I passed. They were all locked. Whatever building this was, retail or office space, this stairwell didn't have access to the interior. Everything was locked from the other side. But what building *was* this? And how had Ivan gotten inside? I wanted to get to an elevator, but I didn't know where Ivan was heading.

Then I realized where he was headed: *the roof.*

With the size of the building we were in, there would be too many exits to cover from the outside, too many rooftop paths to other buildings and escape routes that let out on the ground into small alleyways. With just the single police unit below us having no idea what it was up against, there'd be no way to cover all the possibilities.

It was up to me; down to the two of us. And maybe that was how it'd always been. Maybe that was exactly how I wanted it. This was my shot, the closest I had been.

We were going higher, possibly to a roof way above the streets below. That wouldn't stop me.

I kept running, slowing only now and then to make sure I still heard his feet. I was starting to get winded, but I kept on. The blood pumped in my ears and my stomach felt like hell—fish tacos, fries, and beer were not a good pre-exercise meal—but nothing would get in my way now.

When I stopped again, all was quiet. A quick glance up told me whatever sunlight was above was still some distance away. He wasn't running. I hadn't heard a door slam. He was up there, waiting.

I crept up the next few stairs slowly, angling my gun around and between the bars to have a shot if I saw movement. When I came to the next landing, I crept along the outside wall with my gun aimed up.

My laser sight played a red dot along the walls that I moved carefully from right to left, waiting for it to land on something that wasn't solid.

That was when I felt something brush against my shoulder. I stopped and felt it again. It was a clear, plastic fishing line, set up at about shoulder- or neck-height along the stairs. A small nail held it into the wall on one side and the other end was tied to the handrail. I plucked it with the Glock and felt its tightness. If I'd been running straight on and hit it, it would have cut my neck or at least knocked me down the stairs. But as booby traps went, it wasn't something to kill me.

"Ivan!" I called up the stairwell. "Show yourself, coward."

It was a weak attempt to wound his ego and get him to do something stupid. It didn't work. The stairs remained quiet. I looked up, and estimated we were three or four floors to the roof. Somewhere, Ivan was up there, waiting.

I ducked under the line and stepped slowly along the wall to the next landing, watching for other traps. I could see another door above, likely locked but worth checking. I moved around the wall with caution, playing my sight's laser along the areas that it could reach. I crept up the next flight. At the top, I reached slowly for the door handle, half-expecting Ivan to pop out and knock me back or lunge out at me with his knife.

"Ivan?"

No response, only quiet.

The door was locked like the others. Then something slammed metal against metal above me and a door swung open. All within the stairwell, sirens started to wail, the deafening call of the building's fire alarm—Ivan had broken open a fire exit.

"Fuck," I said under my breath. I started to run.

I careered around the next landing and pumped my knees up the remaining flights of stairs as fast as I could, touching each one instead of skipping steps. I found it easier to keep moving like this. If Ivan had reached the roof, the only thing that would stop him from disappearing completely was me seeing where he went. And that meant I had to get out on the roof, too.

I chugged upward, waving my gun in front of me—both in case I got a shot and to catch any other lines or booby traps. As I came around the last turn, I saw the roof-access door slapping against its frame in the wind. All around me lights flashed and the fire alarm screamed.

At the top I kicked the door with all I had, knocked it back against the wall outside, and lunged out onto the roof's tar surface in a crouch. I spun around 360 degrees, waving my gun, hoping I'd get a shot.

No one was there. Instead, I was out on a narrow walkway across the roof. To either side of me was a large open space. Up above, more of the same building climbed another three or four stories—floors that weren't accessible from our stairwell. I turned and saw the edge of the building in front of me. Beyond that was nothing but air until the other side of the street: thirty yards of open, empty air and, below that, at least fifteen stories down. My breath caught in my throat. My time in the floatplane felt like candy. Nothing would get me closer to that ledge. I backed up until I could feel the wall behind me.

Above were more buildings taller than the one I was on: To my left, the Citigroup tower. Across the street, a gigantic light-gray facade. And to my right, at the far end of this building, across the empty distance of another street, was a third building taller than the others. My knees weakened, but I willed myself forward.

Right or left: I had no idea which way Ivan had gone. I played a hunch and chose right.

CHAPTER 54

I ran across the roof, keeping one hand in contact with the wall and staying away from the edge.

I came to the end and prepared to go around the corner carefully, leading with my gun first, as every agent is taught their first year. This would be Ivan's logical point of ambush, so I moved away from the wall, out toward the ledge. Even if it put me closer to falling, it gave me an extra split second to react if Ivan charged—leaving more room between me and a possible hiding spot. If I had a moment to react, even a moment, that would be enough. I came around the corner and ducked, rolled for extra precaution—fuck the clothes!—but Ivan wasn't there. Thank God.

Then I saw the wall. In front of me now, on the long side of the building's continued rise, was a single word painted in neat, black, block letters: *Equitable*.

In the middle of the word was a ladder that led up the remaining three floors to the roof. Ivan was climbing the ladder, pulling his long body up it at a steady pace.

"Ivan!" I called. "Stop!"

I raised my gun and sighted along its barrel. At this distance the laser's dot was too hard to make out. I didn't have a good shot, but I didn't have any choice other than to fire and show I was serious. Ivan didn't stop.

I shot, and I hit the wall. Ivan looked back and shook his head, then kept going. For a moment I thought he would come down and have it out with me right there, his knife against my gun, and I liked those odds. He didn't, though; he kept climbing. I ran at the ladder, holding my gun on him. He kept getting higher. When he was ten feet from the ladder's top, I yelled again for him to stop.

He didn't.

So I shot—twice. This time, the first shot went off the metal of the ladder just above him, hit brick, and ricocheted into the abyss. Maybe I was aiming there to scare him, maybe I was aiming there to save myself from killing a man. Then the second shot hit home, driving into the back of Ivan's thigh. He stopped for a moment, his head reared back in pain, and he slipped down a few rungs. At that moment I knew I didn't care: if I shot him and he fell, I could live with the consequences, even his death. As his leg lost its strength, he caught himself and began pulling higher with just one leg and his arms.

I'd drawn blood. I moved for the ladder and then stopped. If he got to the roof and went down a staircase through another door, I'd lose him unless he left a trail of blood. Maybe even then. He'd be moving slowly now, but if he got to an elevator, that wouldn't matter. I looked up: he'd slowed, but he was still too far above me to catch him before the roof.

I stepped back to get the best angle and raised my gun. I thought of the women I'd seen left in their apartments, what he'd done to them, and what he'd forced me to witness, the images I'd never forget. I thought about Trent and Oscar and young Vitali left skinned in the woods, and I thought of the files I'd only just started reading about women in other countries.

I sighted up, aimed at his back, his right shoulder, reasoning that if I took out the leg and the arm on that same side, he'd have one hell of a hard time climbing.

For a moment, I thought I could see the laser against his back. Then he came above the shaded space on the wall to a point where the sun shone directly onto him, and the dot was gone. The day was well into afternoon now, San Francisco's sun at its brightest. Ivan was enveloped in daylight, just the way he liked it.

I squeezed the trigger and fired. His body shuddered, and he stopped. It looked as though I'd hit him square in the back, just under his shoulder blade. He writhed, hugged himself against the ladder, and then shook out his arm. He didn't look down, just kept pulling himself up with the other hand. I fired again and hit him again. He kept climbing. He was only a few rungs from the top of the ladder now. I shot to kill but missed.

Finally he stopped, looked back at me and down, and for a moment I thought he was going to leap through the air, knife out, spiraling down to crush and stab me from above. Something in his face shone with that much malice and pain that I could believe he'd jump down three floors to attack me. I confess that I flinched.

I stepped back, altering my final shot just enough that I missed again. In that instant, he pulled himself up the last two rungs and threw his body over the edge of the *Equitable* sign onto the roof.

He was gone.

CHAPTER 55

My knees wobbled from looking up so high. I started toward the ladder, gun in hand, ready to climb as fast as I could. Ivan Nikolaevsk was mine, and I wasn't going to let him get away no matter how I felt about heights.

I'd shot him three times now; he'd be slow to move, trailing blood, but he'd move if I left him up there. I was going to catch him, get my man, no matter what.

I hit the ladder and started climbing, telling myself it was just like my mother's fire escape that summer or like the climbing wall in Project Adventure; as long as I didn't have to jump for the trapeze, I'd be fine.

I felt my pulse increase, my heart pounding, and that cocaine feeling of racing fear in my blood. I still had to climb. Intellectually, I knew the fear didn't make sense: that nothing would overtake my mind and convince me to jump; I would *not* let go of the ladder. I knew I never would, but that was my fear: that I would simply let go. There it was: this was my fear.

I pushed myself up each rung, hanging on with my hands and wrapping my legs around the supports as I went. Above me I saw the ladder against the black wall and felt strong winds blow against my body. I wasn't going to look down or out toward the street. I wouldn't let go of the ladder, would not let myself fall. I climbed. The ladder was maybe thirty feet up—three floors. I scrambled up the first ten with my gun in my right hand, and then switched it to my left. My fingers felt better now—I had so much adrenaline flowing through me that I couldn't even feel them—and my right hand wasn't bandaged. Instead it felt slick with sweat. The wind howled and whipped through my hair, funneled at me by the high-rise caverns and across the tops of buildings.

At each rung, I tried to hold onto the metal as tightly as I could. I stopped twice to dry my hands, wiping them on my pants. I wrapped my legs as I'd been told in junior high school, one leg in front, one behind. I did the same with my hands, gripping the rungs with my palms facing toward me, as if I was doing pull-ups.

The flats I wore had slippery bottoms, leather soles, and again they weren't the shoes for the job. I should have gone barefoot long ago, perhaps, but instead of kicking my shoes off now, I kept moving. I feared that if I kicked them off, I'd hear how long it took them to fall.

The imaginary sound of a shoe hitting the roof below echoed in my head, sending a chill over my skin.

I closed my eyes for a moment, willing myself not to look down, and took two slow, deep breaths with my forehead resting against a cold metal rung. Then I thought of Ivan dragging his bloody leg onto an elevator, going into a building, and never being seen again until he wanted me to find him.

That couldn't happen. I didn't want to go through life watching and wondering where he might be or when he'd show up. Whether I let myself be a normal human being or didn't, I'd have to worry about him everywhere. I'd never be normal like that. Never happy. No, that wasn't going to happen. I wouldn't let it.

I climbed on. Pushing myself to go faster, looping my arms and legs around the ladder, grabbing at the rungs. As I got near the top, I switched the gun back to my right hand. It was only a couple more rungs now. I didn't see him. The wind was too loud to hear even my own voice. I half-expected his head to pop over the wall and him to attack me. I knew I couldn't stop. I went right to the top of the ladder and put my hand up over the ledge to pull myself over.

That was when I felt the greatest pain I'd ever felt, as Ivan stabbed his big hunting knife through the back of my left hand.

CHAPTER 56

Everything went black for an instant. I pulled away, arched my back away from the ladder. My other hand went free and one of my feet slipped off its rung. I fell and only one of my feet caught. I might have slipped off the ladder completely if it weren't for the knife stuck into my hand, keeping it in place. I felt my flesh pull against the blade. It cut me even more.

I scratched at the wall with my right hand, holding the gun and scraping it against the painted bricks. My other foot caught a rung. I wrapped my leg around the ladder and held on with both thighs clenched.

"How does it feel, Agent Harding? To know that you might die."

He pushed the knife through my hand, turning it a bit, and I screamed. I bit my cheek to try to keep myself from blacking out.

Ivan's lips snarled, gleaming red with his own blood.

I stepped one foot up another rung, winding my leg around the back of the ladder to wedge it between the bars and the wall, and pushed my left hand up, trying to free it from the knife.

"Does this hurt, Harding?" He turned the knife again.

With my right hand I was doing my best to hold the ladder *and* the gun. It felt like I was doing a good job of neither. Whatever damage from the cut, the cold of the wind, the fear of the climb and the way I'd fallen, I had just the barrel of the Glock pinned in my hand against the ladder's support. It faced left, away from any direction that mattered, not that I could get a finger on the trigger if I wanted.

"What would happen if I pulled this out, Jess?"

A drop of blood slipped off Ivan's chin and landed on my arm. I could see it seep into the fabric of my coat. He pulled the knife out, held it up and let my hand fall. I grabbed at the top rung with it, but the hand didn't hold; my fingers wouldn't move. The hand just bounced off the metal. I couldn't feel it at all.

I ground my teeth. Ivan was just three feet above me and there was nothing I could do.

"Maybe I cut your other hand now," he said, reaching out over the roof with his knife, leaning toward my right hand. "Maybe I even take your gun, Jess. How would you like that?"

"Fuck you, Ivan."

"Yes. I would like that, you know?"

"I'd do it," I said. "Just tell me why."

He paused. "Why?"

I wrapped my left arm around a rung, wove my forearm through another. My legs were weak from clinging to the ladder, but I could hold now. Ivan stayed where he was, hanging down over me with his knife ready, poised over my right hand and the gun. All he had to do was cut me there and the gun would fall.

"Why always the white nights and the sunlight?" I asked. "Tell me what it is that makes you kill them then."

He smiled for a moment, took his eyes off my hand to look me in the eyes. It had been what he wanted me to ask him all along.

"Yes," he said. "You see now."

That was when I let go of the ladder with my right hand and got a good grip on the gun. The four inches between the ladder and the wall was enough space to aim and shoot; I pointed the gun right up at Ivan's face and pulled the trigger. I couldn't even hear the sound.

His head rocked back and blood spurted up out of his forehead into the air. That part of his face just burst open. Then his head fell forward against the wall and blood poured from his mouth and nose. I got my arm up in time to block it from falling in my face. I climbed one rung higher and pushed his head back up over the wall, onto the roof.

He was gone.

Wind howled around me, chilled me, and shook me against the wall. The ladder trembled. My feet and legs hurt; one of my hands ached, and I couldn't feel the other at all. I closed my eyes for a moment, wondering if any part of me wanted to let go and just fall. If there was something inside me that wanted to do this, that I needed to fear, I was ready for it to take over now.

"Take me," I said. "Here I am."

Nothing happened. Battered and tired and injured, my body still did what I meant it to do. I knew exactly what I wanted. I climbed up the last rungs of the ladder and got myself over the top of the wall onto the roof. There I saw Ivan laid out on his back, a pool of his own blood spreading like a halo from his head. But he was no angel and it didn't bother me one bit that he was gone. Better him than me. That was the only way I could see it in that moment.

He lay on that roof in the brisk sunlight; it was clear and bright as day. He would never move again, never harm another woman. The knife had fallen out of his hand and it lay next to him until I kicked it away, knocking off drops of my own blood. I stood over him, watching his lifeless body, making sure he didn't breathe. All of us were better off.

EPILOGUE

After a blood transfusion and some time in the hospital, Linstrom turned out to be okay. He lived. Ivan had injected him with an animal tranquilizer, etorphine, which knocked him out but also slowed his heart rate and the flow of blood. He turned out lucky, too, in that he had a common enough blood type to make a transfusion routine.

In the weeks that followed, he got better and stronger. The San Francisco office of the Bureau officially brought him in on a temporary transfer so he no longer had to use his vacation time or sick leave to be there.

I got a strong reprimand for my role in this. I had pursued the Daylight Killer in San Francisco without telling anyone, brought in another agent from outside the office without approval or notification, and hadn't procured sufficient backup to keep us each from getting hurt. All of this set me up for a two-month mandatory leave without pay.

I didn't care.

We kept Roberts's name out of it. After all, what did she know other than I had a hot date and needed to let off some steam? She knew I was wound too tight, but so did everyone else in the office.

I needed the extra time to think everything through. Call it a mental recovery holiday, but I also needed surgery on my left hand and had to start physical therapy on my right. In addition to the scarring, I would lose my full range of motion if I didn't work at it. Sometimes this seemed like a full-time job, or as much of one as I could handle.

Once Linstrom was in better shape, we both flew back to Anchorage. No one cared where I did my leave, and they have physical therapists there, believe it or not—ones just as good as those in San Francisco.

Anchorage was his idea, of course, his home, and he wanted me close by. He wanted to spend time together doing things like traveling, going to museums. Everything we did felt like a date. I wasn't sure how that grabbed me.

When he told me he loved me, I still didn't know. September would come, and we'd decide to go back to San Francisco for the Bay Area summer together or not. I was no longer afraid either way—I didn't think. Sleeping with him made me happy, and in the rest of the ways a man and a woman can be together we did just fine.

I had shot a man in the line of duty, a hard thing for an agent both administratively and emotionally. In that way maybe I was human like anybody else. The Bureau bought my self-defense explanation without batting an eye but enforced the mandatory counseling that goes along with any shooting death in the field. I thought this was bullshit of the first order but agreed anyway. What could I do? They wanted me to talk, so I talked.

I went to counseling, did physical therapy on my hand, waited for my surgery to heal, and tried to love Linstrom. I was trying to be a normal.

A lot had transpired between Ivan and me through the wall that separates good and evil. Believe it or not, that wall has cracks—plenty of them. My counselor has tried to examine it, spell the thing out, but I know what happened is better off left unsaid and unexamined, at least for now.

All I knew was I had scars on both hands and some on my heart as well. Ivan only had a scar on one hand, but now he was dead. Someday I might lose the part of me that became connected to him, the piece of my mind that helped me know where he was on that final day. I figured it would free itself up around the same time I stopped seeing images of his murders when I closed my eyes. All I could do until then was wait, regardless of what the Bureau prescribed.

Ivan was dead before they got him down off the roof. My shot went through his jaw from close range, then up and out through the top of his head. With a .40-caliber slug at that distance, the outcome was assured. I wish I could say I felt better about it all, that killing him got my rage out, but it didn't. The balancing act doesn't work that way, and neither do Justice's scales.

That's never been the nature of this work. Maybe there was never any way to mete out an adequate punishment for his crimes. You do what you can and hope the chips fall in your favor—with enough of the people you care about still okay in the end and the bad people out of commission.

I have a few beers with Martinez on occasion, call him René as much as possible, and break his balls every which way so he always knows who has seniority. He says he wants to transfer to San Francisco and come work with me there. We'll have to see about that.

I've been hearing from Roberts that my name is spoken well of in the halls and around the water cooler at the San Francisco office— that I've gotten some cult status as the agent who broke all the rules in the path to getting her man. They say I'm some kind of hero.

My name has come up in conversations regarding promotions, even department leadership. There's also a huge round of budget cuts coming, though, and talk about sharing agents with the SFPD to help with their investigations—to keep the streets clean. Maybe that would be best for me: a change of scenery and direction, cases on a smaller scale and more ability to help the city. God knows it needs it.

They say working with the police would give me more cases and maybe I like that idea; maybe being less single-minded would do me well.

I mentioned all this to Martinez, thinking it would turn him off from coming south, but he said that even if I go to the police for a few years, he wants to come down and stay with me. I'm not so sure.

As for Linstrom coming back to San Francisco, I really don't know. If he and I stay together, who knows? Maybe we'd be good for each other. He says he likes the Bay Area. I've heard of crazier things than me being in a real relationship for the long term. Not many, but some.

I haven't gone back to see any of the old crime scenes in Alaska. We can drive east along the Glenn Highway, see the Matanuska Glacier from a distance, even drive up to Denali and Fairbanks in search of longer days, more sunlight, and bigger mountains, but I'm not going back toward Homer or anywhere near Nikolaevsk.

Even if I owe Alexandra for her help and maybe even like her, I'll never volunteer to tell her what happened to Ivan or Vitali. My debt will have to remain unpaid. I don't want her to see my hands. Not the double scars of their shamed exiles and wrongdoers. If Ivan gave me their mark of damnation, I'm not going where that vocabulary holds meaning.

I've talked to doctors about plastic surgery. Anyone I consult with tells me it's better to wait and let my cuts heal a little more, so I do.

In bed at night, under the gray-dawn Alaskan sun, my palms itch and burn from their own heat. I don't say anything about it to Oscar. I just lie awake on top of the sheets, listening to him breathe next to me as he sleeps like an innocent.

With my eyes open or shut, I see Ivan and think of him, remember the letters and words he scrawled in blood across the apartments of women he murdered and left behind. I think of all the maimed bodies and I think of Trent. I played a role in his death and I still can't forgive myself for that.

I did find my man and bring him to justice—if not the justice of the US legal system, then one that Ivan didn't have any choice about recognizing, one that spans all the countries where he killed women. In the manner that it ended, I can see a certain logic and make a peace with it, if only for myself.

Ivan went out in a way that he and the people of Nikolaevsk and the souls of the dead women would understand, a way that seems fitting with the laws and the order of the Great Land.

When I hear Linstrom breathing next to me at night, I know I saved his life and others' lives by what I did, with the rules I broke and the risks I took. If nothing else, this should make it all worthwhile in the end.

Anyway, I hope it does.

ACKNOWLEDGMENTS

First off, thanks to Kelly for accompanying me on the trip to Alaska that wound up being the inspiration and research expedition for this book. I would never have gone there without you, and I couldn't have dreamed up a better traveling partner for the "Great Land." As with this, in many things you are the partner that I have long dreamed of. You teach me new things every day, and I look forward to each next one together. We're starting an incredible new journey this year with Willa. I wouldn't want to take it with anyone else.

Thanks to Stacia for making this venture with Thomas & Mercer happen. She proves again and again that the old agent model stills work when you're with the right person. I owe so much to her for the tireless support, reading, and for being the best partner-in-pens that a writer could ask for. She's amazing; she rocks.

Thanks so much to the crew at T&M: Jeff Bell for first agreeing, and then Andy, Jacque, Reema, Daniel, Gracie and Justin for bringing this all the way through to the finish. From the times at Bouchercon and every step of the way, it has been a great pleasure. You are the publisher every writer wants. Here's to the future!

Thanks for reading early drafts of the manuscript to Jim and Shawna. Eric Campbell, Aldo Calcagno, and Mark Coggins have believed in my work in ways that inspire me to work harder in attempts to deserve what they see. Lee Dal Monte and Gary Johnson gave countless hours of assistance with sound editing.

Amazing! Paul Rogalinski and Jason Andrews never asked for a thing for maintaining my websites and online presence with skill, grace, and kindness always. Thanks so much to all of you.

Much love to my family: Dad, Mom, and Margot; Jessica the wunderkind; Palms Uncle Stu and his crew in Michigan; Aaron, Tanner, and Deb; Sheila and Lester; Lisa, Luis, Sammy, and Mia; Ruth and Stan (plaid on plaid); the Faigels and the Williamsons. To my new family: Jason, Linda, Jim, Bruce, and the whole San Francisco crew. All of you help me make my world.

To my teachers and students: Thanks for giving your time to help me learn to write *and* for inspiring me with the writing you do. I'll keep working at that balance!

Finally, to *the Palms Family*, all of you out there who listened, read, posted, promoted, encouraged, and helped to spread the word. Thanks for being my first audience. I can't wait to give you more stories!

Last but not least, here's to Willa, my little peanut, my beauty, the light in my eyes.

ABOUT THE AUTHOR

Born in Boston, Massachusetts, Seth Harwood has been a commodities floor trading clerk, bartender, high school teacher, creative writing instructor, English teacher, and rare book cataloguer. He grew up playing basketball, then went on to DJ for his college radio station at Washington University, before attending the Iowa Writers' Workshop, where he earned an MFA in fiction writing. The author of *Jack Wakes Up*, *This Is Life–A Jack Palms Novel*, *A Long Way from Disney*, and *Young Junius*—and named a Best of 2010 author by George Pelecanos—Harwood makes his home in San Francisco, where he teaches creative writing and English at City College of San Francisco and Stanford.

18774319R00143

Made in the USA
Charleston, SC
20 April 2013